"You focus on getting to the car, got it?"

"You'd better keep up, Michaelson, because I'm not leaving without you."

Gray arched a brow. "Yes, ma'am."

Sweat trickled beneath Cat's collar and between her shoulder blades. *God, it's me—I'm trusting You to lead us and guide us, to not forsake us.*

They sprinted across the blacktop. She heard the ensuing commotion, the shouts and gunning of an engine. The unmistakable sound of a gunshot blasted her ears, and she ducked.

"Don't stop!" Gray commanded.

He crouched near the trunk and returned fire. The bullet pinged off their bumper.

Cat jammed the key into the lock. "Let's go," she urged.

Diving inside, she reached across and tugged the lock on his side. Gray dropped onto the seat, slammed the door and rolled down the window.

She gunned the heavy car into Reverse and got a glimpse of the guard lying prone on the ground, blood pooling around him. Nausea swirled, and a moan of denial escaped.

The van roared off the curb and rocketed toward them...

Karen Kirst was born and raised in east Tennessee near the Great Smoky Mountains. She's a lifelong lover of books, but it wasn't until after college that she had the grand idea to write one herself. Now she divides her time between being a wife, homeschooling mom and romance writer. Her favorite pastimes are reading, visiting tearooms and watching romantic comedies.

Books by Karen Kirst

Love Inspired Suspense

Explosive Reunion
Intensive Care Crisis
Danger in the Deep
Forgotten Secrets

Visit the Author Profile page at Harlequin.com for more titles.

FORGOTTEN SECRETS

KAREN KIRST

LOVE INSPIRED SUSPENSE

INSPIRATIONAL ROMANCE

LOVE INSPIRED® SUSPENSE
INSPIRATIONAL ROMANCE

ISBN-13: 978-1-335-72194-5

Recycling programs for this product may not exist in your area.

Forgotten Secrets

This is a work of fiction. Names, characters, places and incidents are either the product of the author's imagination or are used fictitiously. Any resemblance to actual persons, living or dead, businesses, companies, events or locales is entirely coincidental.

This edition published by arrangement with Harlequin Books S.A.

For questions and comments about the quality of this book, please contact us at CustomerService@Harlequin.com.

Love Inspired
22 Adelaide St. West, 40th Floor
Toronto, Ontario M5H 4E3, Canada
www.Harlequin.com

Printed in U.S.A.

Be strong and of a good courage, fear not, nor be afraid of them: for the Lord thy God, he it is that doth go with thee; he will not fail thee, nor forsake thee.
–Deuteronomy 31:6

To my readers—thank you for the emails, messages and notes. Your appreciation for my stories and characters keeps me typing.

ONE

The hollow crack of a gun discharge pulled Sergeant Catriona Baker off her screened-in porch, across the yard and onto the short dock. This section of the river formed a natural cove, and her rental cottage had an unobstructed view of the sprawling town park. Old-fashioned lampposts stationed around the bathrooms emitted enough light for her to make out a violent scene. Multiple armed shadow figures converged on their chosen victims—a man and woman in the wrong place at the wrong time. They seized the woman and began propelling her toward a waiting sedan. Her screams reached across the water and clawed at Cat's conscience, urging her to act. The man's valiant attempts to prevent the abduction were unsuccessful. The first blow from a crowbar knocked the gun from his hand. The second one felled him.

Cat flinched. Had that been a fatal blow?

The men shoved the woman into the back

seat and climbed in beside her. The tires burned against the pavement. Where were they taking her? Would they let her live?

Cat's tennis shoes became unglued from the dock, and she bolted into the cottage. Her gun was in the safe in her bedroom closet. It seemed to take ages to punch in the code. With her Glock in hand, she sprinted outside to her '72 Chevelle. The trip to the park entrance usually took five minutes. She made it in two.

Driving through the deserted park, with speed bumps jarring the wheels and metal frame, she ignored the warning pulsing through her mind. The last time she witnessed a crime, doing the right thing had backfired. Getting involved in someone else's mess had almost ended her military career. She had no family and only a handful of trusted friends, so the Marine Corps was her entire life, and the marines she served alongside were her brothers and sisters. It had taken years to rebuild her reputation and regain her professional footing. She wouldn't jeopardize that again.

This isn't Okinawa. People's lives are hanging in the balance now.

Cat couldn't simply contact emergency services and return to her comfortable porch chair and jazz records while an injured stranger lay alone on a deserted patch of pavement.

As she rounded the curve into the riverside area, her headlights skimmed a new-model Cadillac SUV and, beside it, a man who lay motionless in a pool of blood. This wasn't the one she'd seen from the dock. She slammed on the brakes. Killing the engine, she reached for her phone, but it wasn't in the console. In her rush to reach the scene, she'd forgotten it.

She hadn't forgotten her Glock. The familiar weight in her hand, she threw open the door and ran to the Cadillac. There was little chance he'd survived the head shot. Still, she searched for a pulse and found none. A knot of regret tangled in her midsection. Leaving the victim, she hurried on to the shadowed area beyond the bathrooms. There, the man she'd seen from her dock lay sprawled in the grass. Cat sank to her knees and leaned over him. The reassuring puffs of air against her cheek felt like a victory. Resting on her heels, she tucked her gun in her waistband and took hold of his wrist. Pulse was strong and even. Cat performed a quick assessment. Aside from the nasty gash near his temple, he didn't appear to have any other injuries.

"Who are you?" she murmured, gently lowering his arm to the ground.

The stranger's three-piece suit, starched shirt and shiny loafers pointed to a career in business. His triathlon-ready physique spoke of a more active lifestyle. A chunky, all-terrain watch with more gadgets than her phone supported the second observation. In fact, she was getting a military vibe from him. His wavy brown hair was far from military-cut regulation, though.

Government agent, maybe? Organized crime member? Private security?

She really needed to contact the authorities. Not only to handle him and report the dead man, but to rescue the woman.

Cat searched his jacket pockets first. If she couldn't find his phone, she'd have to return home for hers. Leaving him alone was out of the question. But moving an injured person was a no-no, unless they were in imminent danger. Besides, she doubted she could get him into her car unassisted.

His lashes fluttered and his lips moved. "Sir, can you hear me? What's your name?"

He grunted something that sounded like "bee."

She placed her hand lightly against his shoulder. "I'm here to help you. I need to call for an ambulance. Do you have a phone?"

His eyes opened to slits, and she could only see they were dark and unfocused. "Bee."

The word made no sense. Unless he was actually saying Bea, short for Beatrice, as in perhaps the woman who'd been taken. The sense of urgency renewed, she patted the outer side of both pant pockets and discovered what she was looking for.

"I'm going to remove your phone, sir," she told

him. He didn't appear to have heard her, because he had gone silent again.

A grim prospect occurred to her as she dialed 911. Had the blow to his head caused a brain bleed?

God, it's me, Cat. Catriona Baker. She winced. He knew her name. The name her birth mother had given her before leaving her on a social worker's doorstep.

You know I don't bother You unless absolutely necessary.

She'd put her faith in Christ years ago. It made sense that she'd handle what she could on her own and bother Him with the big stuff. She studied the man's pale countenance.

This is one of those times. I don't know what this man did to deserve this. Maybe he got involved with a dishonest crowd or angered the wrong criminal. Maybe he's innocent and trouble sought him out. Whatever the case, please don't let me be the last person he sees alive.

He didn't regain consciousness during the interminable wait for the ambulance. Cat stayed beside him, alert for the possible return of the men responsible for tonight's chaos. Sometimes criminals acted according to a common script. Other times, they shredded and burned the script. Those were the times law enforcement officers were tested to their limits.

When the paramedics arrived, she watched silently as they strapped him to a gurney. The police cruisers' headlights cast his features in harsh relief. Sitting in the dark with him, watching his chest rise and fall, she'd imagined a variety of scenarios. He and the missing woman could be married. He wasn't wearing a ring, but some men chose not to. They could be engaged. Or related somehow.

She'd been tempted to scroll through his phone. A simple press of his thumb would've given her access, but she couldn't bring herself to invade his privacy. Growing up in the foster care system, she'd had scant little of that. Now she guarded her own and respected others'.

They loaded him into the ambulance and closed the doors. The decision to follow wasn't well thought out, but she wouldn't get a wink of sleep without knowing his prognosis. She skirted the officers processing the scene and allowed herself only a quick glimpse of the medical examiner going about his job. Was the deceased man a friend or enemy of the couple? As a military police officer assigned to a smaller installation, she dealt mostly with domestic disputes, impaired drivers and thefts. She'd seen a dead body before—her favorite foster dad had collapsed and died at the dinner table. The violence of this death was very different. She hoped the men responsible were brought to justice.

Having already given her statement and contact information to the first officer on the scene, Cat didn't tell anyone she was leaving. Doubts assailed her as she once again navigated dark, empty streets. It was going on 2300 hours, and she had to report for her shift in six hours. She should go home and get updates on the morning news like the rest of the coastal North Carolina community.

Instead, she drove to the hospital in Jacksonville and waited for more than two hours in the crowded ER waiting room. Hospital staff had told her only that he was awake and coherent and not ready for visitors. Cat had decided to go home and was almost to the exit when her friend Audrey Tan passed through the patient-area doors in her surgical scrubs.

"Cat." Audrey left her coworker's side and strode over. "Are you here for medical care?"

She explained the situation. "I'd hoped to get an update before I left, but I'm not a friend or family member."

Audrey didn't act surprised during the unusual account. She'd endured much worse at the hands of an organized crime boss. "I'll find out for you. Wait here."

She was gone long enough for Cat to wonder if she'd been called away on another surgery. When Audrey reappeared, she beckoned for Cat to follow.

"I'm taking you to him."

"I didn't ask to see him."

"He's asking to see you."

"I'm certain he doesn't remember me."

The dip between Audrey's brows pinched. "That's the problem. He doesn't remember anything."

"Meaning the details of the attack are fuzzy?"

Stopping at a corner room, Audrey nodded to the closed door. "Worse. He has retrograde amnesia."

TWO

Shock rippled through Cat. Amnesia? Her mind replayed the moments prior to him being robbed of his identity and life history.

"Images revealed mild structural damage to his brain, which would account for the memory loss," Audrey explained.

"Will he need surgery?"

"No, but he will require observation and monitoring overnight." She paused. "He gave me permission to divulge this information."

"Why would he do that? I'm a stranger."

"Everyone is a stranger. But, Cat, you saw tonight's events unfold. You're the one person who can help him make sense of what's happened."

The pronouncement stole her breath. She didn't want to play any role, let alone a pivotal one, in a situation of this magnitude.

Audrey clasped her shoulder. "Just talk to him. Satisfy his curiosity. You decide how involved you'll get."

The understanding in her gaze soothed most of Cat's worries. She wasn't at the mercy of anyone else's whims or dictates. She controlled what happened next.

Squaring her shoulders, she thanked her friend and entered the room alone. The man in the hospital bed was older than the guys she worked with, early to midthirties, if she were to guess. His rich brown hair, thick and tousled, framed thoughtful, intense features.

"Miss Baker?" His stormy blue eyes threatened to tug her into his nightmare. "You're the witness?"

Forcing her feet into motion, she walked toward him and stopped at the foot of his bed, projecting the air of nonchalance that had carried her through the grueling months of boot camp and the Law Enforcement Military Police course.

"It's Sergeant Baker," she stated. "I'm stationed at the New River Air Station, a few miles from Camp Lejeune."

"A marine." Admiration tinged his deep voice. "Thank you for your service."

She hadn't been expecting that. "Your accent is familiar. Like mine, actually. I'm from the Chicago suburbs."

His jaw clenched. "The nurse told you about my current problem?"

Cat looked away from the desolation in his eyes. The machines attached to him emitted readings that danced across multiple screens. She hadn't had a storybook childhood, but worse would be to remember nothing.

"Yes, she did."

"I need for you to walk me through tonight's ambush."

The quiet command brought her gaze back to him. His quest for answers revolved around her. She would give him what he wanted and wish him all the best.

His brain had suffered bruising, they'd told him. The area that stored memories had been damaged, and no one could say for sure if he'd ever recover them. His mind was like a faulty map with no identifiers and no coordinates.

He glanced at the IV tubes taped to his hand and considered tearing them out and bolting. But where would he go? He didn't know the hospital layout, much less how to navigate a town he'd never seen. The police hadn't found his wallet. He had no name, no Social Security number, no history. He was a homeless, penniless John Doe.

The ache he'd tolerated since regaining consciousness curled around his skull and squeezed like a merciless python. Closing his eyes, he pinched the bridge of his nose and focused on his breathing. In and out. Clearing his lungs and purging the agitation.

There was hope in the midst of this catastrophe. A witness.

"I was relaxing on my screened-in porch, listening to Diana Krall," she said.

The young woman's stance projected confidence. A pink T-shirt advertising Topsail Beach overlapped black leggings. Pristine black-and-white tennis shoes adorned her feet. Her flamered hair was restrained in a thick bun. Thanks to her pert nose and abundance of freckles, he didn't quite buy the air of complete composure. Then her silver-green eyes cut through him like a laser, and he reassessed that impression.

"What's your first name?"

"Catriona."

"Nice to meet you, Catriona. I'd return the favor, but I don't know mine." The quip was meant to relax her. Stress would hinder her ability to remember vital details.

She grimaced. "Your phone will surely shed light on your identity. I used it to contact EMS. I didn't unlock it."

He nodded, thinking if she'd been nosier, he might have a name to go with his face. He might also know the abducted woman's identity. Frustration marched beneath his skin like a troop of fire ants. His hands fisted in the lightweight sheet covering him.

"Do you have it with you?" he asked.

"I gave it to an officer. I didn't know I'd be coming here."

"I'm grateful you did." He had to work hard to form a smile, and he wasn't sure he was successful. Smiling didn't feel natural. "I should've said this straight off—thank you for coming to my aid."

She blushed. "I stayed with you until the paramedics came. That's it."

"What you did was extremely brave and kind."

She cleared her throat. "I should finish the story so you can rest. I heard the gun report and went to investigate. The cottage I rent has an unobstructed view of the park."

"What time was this?"

"About 2145. I saw men—"

"How many?"

"Three, I think, not counting the driver. Two flanked the woman. The other one attacked you." Standing at attention, she smoothed the edges of her shirt. "He struck you twice with the crowbar. The first blow knocked the gun from your grasp."

His fingers went to the nasty bruises on his right forearm, and her gaze followed. "Is it broken?"

"The X-ray didn't show evidence of a fracture. My skull is intact, though I'm told my brain probably bounced around a little."

"Ouch. I'm guessing you have a doozy of a headache."

He lifted the hand where the IV was attached. "Intravenous Tylenol works wonders. They wouldn't give me something with more kick, since they had no knowledge of my medical history…"

"You could have allergies."

"Yes."

"Your wallet wasn't with your belongings?"

"No."

Maybe he didn't carry identification because he was skirting the law. The thought inspired an overall feeling of despair. Was he responsible for what happened tonight? Was he the reason a woman was in danger?

"The woman I was with. Can you describe her?"

"Like I told the first officer on the scene, I could only make out that she was of average height and weight and that she had long hair."

Worry churned in her eyes. He was worried, too. He had no idea what the missing woman meant to him, how they were connected. Glancing at his left hand, he searched for a tan line. The absence of one was encouraging—how awful would it be to have memories of his own wife erased? To feel absolutely nothing for a woman he'd chosen to share his life with?

"Were they wearing masks?"

"It was too dark. I couldn't tell."

"Do the police have any theories about the man

who died? The staff here have little information. I was told only that he suffered a shot to the head."

"They didn't share any with me. The CSU will sort through the clues and decide how he fits into the puzzle."

He'd hoped the sergeant's account would uncover a memory or help him gain a clearer perspective. But it was only creating more questions. A man died tonight, and he had no way of knowing if he'd been part of the problem or an innocent caught in the cross fire. The throbbing inside his skull built to an excruciating level. Despite what he'd led Catriona to believe, the low-grade painkiller was working like a Band-Aid on a shrapnel wound. He pinched the bridge of his nose, and to his embarrassment, a groan escaped.

Pleasant scents of lemon and mint wafted over him.

"Should I call for a nurse?"

"No." He gritted his teeth, willing himself to rise above the physical pain.

"It's not a sign of weakness to admit you need help," she said somberly.

"They won't give me anything stronger," he grunted. "Lawsuits, you know."

Slowly lowering his hand to the bed, he rested his head against the pillow. The light overhead winked out. Her thoughtfulness arrowed through his chest and embedded in his heart. He was tempted to reach for her hand.

Who did he normally turn to for support? Did he have friends? Family members who'd fret over his disappearance?

He heard the creak of the sink handle and water trickling into the drain. Her shoes squeaked against the tiles as she tiptoed about the room. The next instant, he felt a cool washcloth settle over his forehead. The arrow burrowed deeper.

"I'll leave you to get some sleep."

He opened his eyes and looked at her. "Stay." It hurt to speak. "Please."

She considered his request. Wavered.

Teeth sinking into her lower lip, she shook her head. "I can't. I hope you find your answers."

Catriona Baker left without a single glance back, taking with her any chance of him recovering his memories.

THREE

Cat parked in her gravel driveway, relieved her shift was over. It had been difficult to focus on work and downright impossible to forget a certain stranger's dilemma. The image of him in that bed last night, trying to mask his pain and humbly asking her to stay, taunted her. Guilt had hounded her ever since she stepped foot outside the hospital.

As a member of the United States of America's fighting force, she'd pledged her life to helping others. Protecting others. As a military police officer, she took that responsibility a step further. In this instance, she'd turned and walked away. She couldn't help but feel she'd failed him.

The scars from Okinawa weren't fresh, but they weren't completely healed, either. When she'd witnessed marines stealing guns and ammo from the armory, she hadn't thought twice about reporting it. She couldn't have known that her immediate superior, the next rung in the chain of command, was in on the thefts. Sergeant Toby Craft had been unrepentant. At first he'd tried to lure her into the operation, promising big pay-outs. She'd refused. But before she could report the crime to someone else, Craft had spread wild rumors about her, claiming she was a spurned admirer and had concocted a story to get him and the others in trouble. He'd produced falsified emails to back up his claim. The tide of opinion against her was such that she hadn't stood up for herself. That would always be her biggest regret.

She stomped up the front porch steps and stopped short. The man from last night was lounging in her plastic coral chair. "Why aren't you in the hospital?"

He lumbered to his feet. "They strongly urged me to stay another night, and I strongly refused."

He was taller than she'd thought. Tall and lean. Not thin, though. The white dress shirt, the same he'd had on last night, was layered over compact muscle. His hair was more tousled and unruly today. The white bandage at his temple contrasted with his sun-kissed skin. He stood with his feet planted far apart, and his chin jutted out, emitting an air of command. She was familiar with the take-charge stance. Was he military, perhaps?

"How did you get here?"

"Taxi." At her continued silence, he tacked on, "Don't worry. The hospital staff didn't give out your information. I had the driver take me to the park first. From that vantage point, I worked out the location of your home."

"Well, that's unsettling."

"I realize I shouldn't have shown up unannounced." Waving his phone in the air, he shrugged. "I don't have your number."

"You got your phone back? That's great."

"It would be if there was any information on it. There's no email account, no bank or social media apps." His mouth twisted. "The police are working with the phone company to get my account information released. With no vital information, I can't access it."

"No Social Security number, no birth date."

"No special password," he continued matter-of-factly.

"What about your contacts list?"

"That's the strangest part. There aren't many—maybe a dozen—and they're all businesses. Leads me to believe it's a phone used for professional purposes only." He consulted his monstrosity of a watch. "It's after business hours. I may be able to reach someone tomorrow."

"That should prove to be an interesting conversation," Cat said. "What are you going to do without your wallet?"

"The nurses took pity on me and collected two hundred bucks to tide me over."

The nurses took pity on him, huh? Imagine that. She wondered if they would've been so generous if he'd been out of shape and sporting a bald spot.

Cat had to give him credit. He clearly wasn't playing the why-me game. He wasn't lounging around the hospital feeling sorry for himself. The man was being proactive—a key military standard—and taking steps to solve his problem. But that had led him to her again. And she wasn't looking to complicate her life.

"I wish I could help you," she said, removing her uniform cover and tucking it under her arm. "I've already told you everything I know."

"Would you mind retelling it again? Maybe another key detail will come to mind."

"I've thought of little else today. Believe me, if there was something new to tell you, I would."

His eyes became hooded. "I understand. Before I go, would you mind taking my number?"

"Yes, of course." She retrieved her phone from the roomy side pocket of her camouflage pants and input his number. On a whim, she texted him her contact information. "I'd like to know if—I mean, when—you regain your memory. And when your friend is rescued."

"You got it."

His stomach rumbled as he began to retreat. She sighed.

"Wait." It was 1730. "Did they feed you dinner?"

"It's fine." He smiled and descended the steps.

"I'll have a taxi driver take me to a fast-food restaurant."

"I have leftover chicken stir-fry. You're welcome to join me."

He turned around. As he considered her offer, sunlight slanted through the pines and bathed him in gold, picking out the mahogany and chestnut strands in his hair. His eyes lightened to a brilliant blue. Cat's heart rate picked up. If she wasn't immune to handsome men's charms, she'd be pulling out her wallet and offering him cash, too.

"Stir-fry sounds great," he said.

"There's a picnic table around back."

Cat let herself inside and locked the door behind her. She quickly changed out of her uniform and into a V-necked shirt, jeans and her black-and-white tennis shoes. The kitchen was out of style and cramped, but she didn't have to share the space with anyone else. Using the lone window above the sink, she checked on her guest. He stood on the dock, hands gripping the railing, staring at the crime scene. Willing his memories to return?

God, it's me again. I don't need anything. I'm asking for— I don't know his name, actually. He *doesn't even know his name.*

Her chest felt tight, and her eyes moist. The emotional reaction startled her.

Please help this man recover what he's lost. Amen.

After reheating the leftovers, she divided the mixture onto two plates and took out a pair of forks. He carried the dishes to the picnic table while she got bottles of lemonade from the fridge. Trees along the riverbank provided plenty of shade, and a light breeze brought relief from the lingering August heat.

"I noticed you were limping."

He waited for her to sit first, then settled across from her. "There are scars on my right knee. The doctor believes I had major surgery on it." He tucked into the food. "This is delicious."

She studied the plate and hoped he wasn't allergic to any of the ingredients. "One of my foster moms, Dana, loved to cook," she said without thought. "She made sure I knew my way around the kitchen."

He lowered his fork. "What happened to your parents?"

Cat didn't typically lead with the foster care subject. Surely she wasn't nervous around him? He was older, sure, with classic movie-star appeal. But she held her own in a male-dominated field on a daily basis.

"I can't answer that." Answers to her past had proved elusive. She held off expressions of sympathy with another question. "What about the SUV? Did the police say who it was registered to?"

He rolled with her change in topic, which she appreciated. "The officer who paid me a visit this morning was more interested in posing questions than answering them." He took a long swig of the tart drink. "My role in what played out isn't clear at the moment. Until it is, they won't share sensitive information with me. The focus is on identifying the missing woman and locating her, as well it should be." He swiped the beads of moisture from the bottle label. "I don't want to believe I'm the reason she's in danger."

Cat didn't want to, either. She used to think she had good instincts. Okinawa had proved she couldn't always trust her gut.

It's just one meal. One meal, and he's gone. For good this time.

If he turned out to be on the wrong side of the law, her reputation and judgment would be called into question again. Aiding and abetting a criminal, albeit unknowingly, wouldn't be overlooked by her superiors. That opportunity to train for the Criminal Investigation Division? Gone.

The phone's shrill ring shattered her thoughts. His brows collided as he studied the screen. Swiping his thumb across, he lifted it to his ear. "Hello?"

Whatever the person said caused his features to shutter and his eyes to darken dangerously. That clearly wasn't a friend on the other end.

"Did you hear me, Michaelson?" The voice was disguised. "The heiress's future is in your hands. Convince Winthrop to pay up, or she dies."

The blood roared in his ears. Michaelson. Had to be his surname.

"Michaelson?"

"I heard you," he muttered. He couldn't let slip that he had no idea what was going on. "I'll do as you say. First, I want proof of life."

His gaze collided with Catriona's, and he activated the speaker option.

"Gray?" A feminine voice shivered through the line. "Are you all right? Ross is dead, isn't he?" A sob mixed with a gasp. "I thought they'd killed you, too."

"I'm fine." He hated that his brain wasn't functioning and couldn't identify her. "Are you hurt?"

He heard voices in the background, urging her to hurry. "They want money. They haven't been able to reach my father." A ragged breath reached them. "Gray, have you seen her?"

The question threw him. "Seen who?"

They heard a sharp cry and a scuffle. Another voice came on. A male. "You have twenty-four hours to get Wayne Winthrop to fork over the ransom money."

The line went dead. A second later, a text came through. He relayed the information aloud.

"They want five million cash placed in a trash receptacle in the Jacksonville City Park." His nostrils flared. "If this Wayne Winthrop guy doesn't comply, his daughter Bianca's body will wash up on a local beach."

The fury that gripped him caught him by surprise. Leaving the table, he strode to the dock and glared across the water. Yellow police tape warned park-goers to keep out. Several people had gathered along the perimeter to gawk.

He didn't remember Bianca, didn't know how she fit into his life. Hearing her voice had brought a realism to what had been, up until this point, an abstract concept. There was a real woman in dire danger, and she knew him. She'd called him Gray.

Catriona warily approached and stopped where the yard met the dock. "We have to contact the police."

He clenched his fists. The action caused his bruised arm to ache. "Yes."

"Are you sure you shouldn't be in the hospital?"

"I'm fine." Truth be told, on a scale from one to ten, the pain in his head would rate a twelve. Being admitted to the hospital would've given him access to medication, but sitting around waiting for others to fix his problems wasn't his style. He'd simply have to work through the pain, like he'd done before.

He mentally paused. Where had that random thought come from? Was it related to his knee surgery?

Those silver-green eyes of hers seemed to miss nothing. "What?"

"Nothing."

She hesitated, then gestured to the cottage. "I've heard the name Wayne Winthrop. Wait here."

She went inside and returned with her laptop.

Motioning for him to follow, she set it on the picnic table and resumed her seat. Her fingers flew across the keyboard. The image of a man in a severe black business suit occupied the screen.

"Recognize him?" Cat angled the laptop toward him.

The man's graying blond hair was cut in a conservative style. His features were unremarkable, but they were set in dour lines. A gold wedding ring was his only piece of jewelry.

"No."

Her fingers returned to the keyboard. Another image greeted him, and the food in his stomach turned to lead.

"Bianca," he surmised. "She's just a kid."

"According to this website, she's twenty." More typing. "The Winthrop name is plastered on several public buildings across Chicago. A library. Hospital wing. Wayne was born into a family dynasty of wealth and privilege. He built on that by branching into real estate and magazine and book publications."

He continued to gaze at Bianca's image. How did they know each other?

"What could we have been doing in North Carolina?" he mused.

"Visiting colleges?" Catriona tapped the screen. "Says here she dropped out after her freshman year. Her mother—" She whistled. "Get this. Her mother was Tabitha Hathaway."

He shrugged.

Her brows winged up to her hairline. "Tabitha Hathaway is one of the best jazz singers in the country. I have three of her records. She kept her stage name after she married Winthrop." The sparkle of excitement winked out. "She died last year in a private plane crash. From the looks of things—" she scrolled through photo after photo of mother and daughter together "—the two were extremely close."

"First she loses her mother. Then she gets abducted for ransom."

"Look at this." Catriona's tone changed.

He leaned over her shoulder for a better look. There he was, standing in the background at a social event that looked like a meet and greet, too far away to be her plus-one.

His pulse ratcheted up a notch as the first puzzle piece snapped into place. "I'm her bodyguard."

Catriona skimmed multiple society magazine articles. "There's nothing here." She keyed in Wayne's name and continued to scan. "Found something. Read this."

The words described a stranger.

"You're in charge of the Winthrops' personal security," she said. "Bianca mentioned the name Ross. She said they killed him. That must've been the initial gunshot that I heard."

"We'll give the name to the police."

"Maybe he worked the security detail with you."

"It's possible." Rescanning the article, he said, "This doesn't say what I did before coming to work for them."

She did a search of his name, weeding through life histories of men with the same name as his. "Personal privacy is clearly a priority for you. I'm not surprised, considering your line of work."

"It's extremely unhelpful now."

The Winthrops had made a mistake in hiring him. They'd put their faith in him, and he'd failed them. Amnesia didn't excuse him from doing his duty. He would do whatever it took to find Bianca and return her to her father safe and sound.

He stuck out his hand. "Thank you for the meal, Sergeant. For everything you've done."

Surprise parted her lips. After shaking his hand, she slid off the bench to face him. "Let me give you a ride to the station."

"I appreciate the offer, but there's no need. I can have a ride here in five to ten minutes, and you can enjoy what's left of your evening."

There was no denying the relief in her beautiful eyes. And no wonder. This wasn't her problem. The sense of connection he'd started to feel was solely because she was the lone witness to his tragedy. She'd done as much as she could to help him. He wouldn't ask any more of her.

FOUR

Cat couldn't help but overhear Gray Michaelson's conversation. The taxi company would send a driver, if he didn't mind waiting an hour.

He ended the call and rubbed his forehead. "I'll try another company."

"How many do you think we have here?" she quipped. "I'll drive you."

"I've already taken up too much of your time."

"It's one ride to the station."

Cat's gaze returned to the open laptop screen dominated by Bianca Winthrop's smiling image. The young woman didn't project the jaded, worldly air that media-hog socialites possessed. Her understated appearance—a dusting of makeup, the romantic, flowing dress and loose strawberry blond waves—imparted innocence and purity. Whether or not that was a calculated tactic, Cat couldn't say.

"The police need to hear about that phone call."

She snapped the laptop shut and picked up her glass.

"There's no use delaying any more than I have to," he agreed. "I appreciate it, Sergeant."

He stacked the plates and carried them as far as the screened-in porch, where she subtly blocked his path. There was no specific reason for her to distrust him. He had a nice name to go with his well-put-together features, and he'd chosen a noble profession—protecting others at the expense of his own safety and comfort. Still, she wasn't ready to let him into her home.

"I'll take those."

Gray glanced between her full hands and the kitchen door, understanding dawning. "I'll set them here—" he tilted his head to the side table "—and go fetch the rest."

She appreciated that he didn't question or make light of her hypervigilance. Soon, the picnic table was cleared and the dishes soaking in the sink. The inside of her Chevelle seemed to shrink with him in the passenger seat. Cat was keenly aware of his body heat and the faint scent of hospital-issued shampoo. Her attention strayed to his profile one too many times as she maneuvered the car onto the lightly traveled road.

His pure blue gaze delved into hers, bold, direct and questioning.

She scolded herself for her unusual reaction.

"Did hearing Bianca's voice or seeing the photographs jar any memories?"

"I wish they had."

Cat knew all about the futility of wishes. Refocusing on the road, she saw a police cruiser up ahead.

"I recognize that officer from last night," she said, tapping the brake. "Do you want to report the call to him?"

Gray shifted forward in the seat. "Let's do it."

Cat followed the cruiser through the park to the crime scene. They caught up to the officer at the yellow tape barrier. He recognized them and let them pass, pointing out the lead detective. The woman was crouched at the water's edge, staring out across the river.

"Detective Pike?" Cat said.

Slowly pivoting, the woman inspected them from behind thick glasses that exaggerated her eyes. Corkscrew curls framed a petite face. "I suppose you're connected to the case if Officer Dunning granted you access."

"I'm Sergeant Baker. That's my home across the way."

"Ah, so you're the witness." She stood to her feet and dusted off her hands. "And you must be our John Doe."

"I've had a call from the abductors," he stated. "The hostage is Bianca Winthrop from Chicago.

Turns out I'm the head of her security detail. The name's Gray Michaelson."

Pike whipped out her phone and started typing. "What are their demands?"

"Five million."

She let out a shrill whistle. "Why would they assume you have access to that kind of cash?"

"Not me. Bianca's father, Wayne Winthrop."

"Why does that sound familiar?"

Cat relayed what she knew about the family, concluding with Tabitha's death.

"I was a fan. Terrible tragedy." The detective nodded, frowning. "You have no idea why you'd bring Miss Winthrop to our area? This is quite a distance from Chicago."

"My memory's been wiped clean. I have no answers for you or anyone else." He clenched his fists. "Do you have an ID for the deceased gentleman?"

"Still waiting on the ME to send me the report."

"Bianca mentioned someone named Ross."

Officer Dunning hurried over. "Some joggers found a discarded wallet."

After slipping on a fresh pair of gloves, Detective Pike inspected the contents.

"Is it mine?" Gray said, inching forward.

"The name and photo match," she said. But instead of giving it to him, she retrieved an evidence bag from her satchel and sealed it inside.

"I'm assuming I have a bank card in there," he said. "I'll need access to my account."

"You'll get it as soon as it's processed. In the meantime, we can all go down to the station and work on getting in touch with Mr. Winthrop."

The detective started walking toward her unmarked car, taking for granted that they'd follow. The lone sign of Gray's annoyance was a telltale twitch beneath his eye.

"Detective Pike," Cat called after her, "I have nothing more to contribute."

"You heard the phone call, didn't you?"

"I can't tell you anything that Mr. Michaelson can't."

She spun around, her eyes as big as an owl's behind the glasses. "What's the problem, young lady? Got a hot date?"

Cat felt her cheeks grow warm. "No date."

"A military exercise early in the morning?"

"No, ma'am."

"Then you'll have no problem coming to the station." Opening her car door, she blinked her great owl eyes. "There's a young woman somewhere out there who needs all the help she can get."

Gray was aware that Sergeant Baker would rather be at home. She was well within her rights to wash her hands of the situation. He also knew she wasn't here because Detective Pike was pushy, but because she respected the law enforcement officer and was genuinely concerned about Bianca.

The police station was buzzing with activity. Desk phones trilled almost nonstop. A giant copier in the corner spit out reams of paper. Officers conversed together in random clusters around the room. Pike loomed over a young officer at his desk, who was staring at his computer screen as she barked into the phone.

"This is an official police matter—" The cord twisted around her as she paced. "I don't have to explain to you what business the Jacksonville PD has with your boss." Another stilted silence. "Sir, listen to me. Get Mr. Winthrop to call me on this number ASAP."

She slammed the phone into its cradle and glared at no one in particular. "Entitled jerk."

Standing a few feet away from Gray, Catriona turned her head and met his gaze. A tiny smile played about her mouth. Strangely, it seemed familiar to him.

His phone rang. Everyone in his immediate vicinity stopped what they were doing. Pike straightened and motioned to the young man, who began typing furiously. She nodded at Gray.

He answered the video call and found himself staring at the blond-haired businessman in the online magazine articles.

"Michaelson, I've been pulled out of a meeting by someone claiming to be with the Jacksonville, North Carolina, PD. Do you know anything about that?"

"Sir, it's Bianca. She—"

"Don't tell me she's not in Chicago," he interrupted, his brows crashing into his nose. "Michaelson, where are you? Are those police officers in the room with you? What's going on?"

"Bianca's been abducted."

Gray braced himself for Winthrop's reaction. He didn't recognize the man. Nothing about his boss released a memory. He didn't know what sort of relationship Winthrop shared with his only offspring, didn't know how he reacted to stress.

"This better be some sort of prank," he bit out. His skin flushed red, and his eyes were hard. "Inform Bianca this isn't going to garner the sort of attention she wants."

"This is no prank. She and I traveled here to coastal North Carolina, where she was then captured by thugs. When they failed to contact you, they reached out to me with ransom demands."

Winthrop glared into the phone. "This is ludicrous. She's put her friends up to this, hasn't she? To cut my trip abroad short."

"Is she in the habit of acting reckless?"

"What kind of question is that?"

"I was attacked during the scuffle. I can't remember anything about my life, including you or Bianca."

"Are you telling me you have amnesia?" he spluttered.

"The men holding her hostage aren't pretending, sir. They threatened to harm her if you don't pay."

"Bianca wasn't happy about my trip." His frown deepened. "She hasn't been happy since her mother died."

Gray was at a distinct disadvantage. He couldn't defend the heiress, couldn't attest to her innocence or guilt. But he had spoken to her on the phone. She hadn't sounded like someone staging this in a silly bid for attention.

"Sir, I'm inclined to believe she's in real danger."

Detective Pike motioned for the phone and introduced herself. "Mr. Winthrop, does your daughter have any love interests? Romantic relationships that might've turned sour?"

"She's been dating Lane Turner for about a year. Don't tell me you're taking this as a serious threat?"

"I can't afford not to. Can you?"

Gray couldn't see the screen, but Winthrop's silence was telling. "What do you want to know?"

"I need the names of the people in Bianca's circle, friends and enemies. People she worked with—"

"My daughter isn't employed. She's involved in several charities."

Pike nodded. "We'll need those organizations, as well, along with any potential threats connected to you. The abductors could be moti-vated by greed or something more complicated."

Beside him, Catriona tried to hide a yawn. He motioned toward the coffee machine, and she fol-lowed without a word.

"You should go home," he told her, pouring a cup of the caffeinated brew and offering it to her.

She declined, her demeanor watchful. "What will you do? Where will you go?"

"I'll get a motel room for the night. Tomorrow, I'll pester them until they return my wallet."

"Mr. Winthrop can supply answers for you."

"Bianca is the focus right now."

Her gaze strayed to Detective Pike. "Keep me updated?"

"Of course."

She extended her hand. "I wish you the best, Gray Michaelson."

This time, saying goodbye to the intriguing marine felt final. There was nothing more she could do for the case. For him.

The thick brew burned his throat on the way down. He deliberately didn't watch her leave. Re-turning to the hub of activity, he noticed Pike had shifted to the windows and had lowered her voice. She glanced his way once before turning her back to him. They were discussing him.

Could he be in on the plot? Maybe he was working behind the scenes to extort money. Was he trustworthy?

Gray funneled his fingers through his hair and gulped more coffee. The headache had returned with a vengeance, and he'd noticed his knee was aching. He hadn't stuck around the hospital long enough to get the full rundown on his condition. He couldn't answer the simplest questions about himself. Did he even like coffee?

Focus. There are bigger things at stake.

God, I'm at a loss. My past is a mystery. I don't know how to help Bianca. Please protect her. Lead the police to her.

As soon as the spontaneous prayer formed, Gray recognized the significance. He was clearly comfortable praying to an unseen God and expected Him to respond. The notion comforted him.

Pike passed the phone off to the officer, who posed more questions to the business mogul.

"I'd like for you to stay close for the time being," she told Gray.

"Did Winthrop vouch for me?" he asked pointblank. "Or am I a suspect?"

"He gave you a sterling review, but you're not entirely in the clear. You're what I call a gray area," she said, smirking. "Winthrop agreed to have his assistant forward your résumé and work up a list of known factors about your life. Let's walk down to Evidence and see if we can at least get your driver's license and credit card. I'll do a quick review of your record to see if you're good to drive. I'm assuming if you're on Winthrop's payroll, you're able to afford a rental car and hotel for the night. See me if that's not the case."

A half hour later, he was free to go. An officer gave him a lift to the closest rental company, where he secured a late-model SUV and got directions to a reputable hotel. He had enough cash to cover one night. Tomorrow, he'd call the bank. He hoped his driver's license information would convince them to let him reset his password.

Instead of driving straight to the hotel, he headed for the park. There was about an hour of daylight left, and he intended to walk the grounds himself for clues the police may have overlooked. More important, he hoped being at the scene might spark a memory.

There were a number of people enjoying the clear summer evening. Gray parked near the bathrooms and ambled toward the water's edge, his gaze scanning the asphalt, sidewalks and grass. A small boat trolled in the cove, and the fishermen's voices traveled across the water's surface.

The buzzing in his pocket startled him. He noticed it was an unknown number, and his stomach twisted.

"Hello?"

"Lane?"

He'd been expecting to hear the altered voice of one of the abductors. Instead, the same panicked female voice he'd heard hours earlier reached out to him. Then he registered the name she'd used. Had she been trying to reach her boyfriend?

"Please tell my father he'll need to cough up extra cash for one of the guards. He agreed to let me call you."

His fingers tightened on the phone.

"Bianca? It's Gray. Where are you?"

"I—I miss you, too, Lane. But you shouldn't worry about me. As long as these guys get their money, I'll be okay."

"Got it. Can you give me any hints where you are?"

"Please tell Catriona I'll be reunited with her soon." A note of warning threaded through her voice.

His damaged brain struggled to process her words. She knew Catriona? How? What message was she trying to convey?

"Is she in danger?"

"Yes."

There was a commotion on the other end, followed by angry voices.

The line went dead. A growl ripping through his chest, he stared at the yellow cottage on the opposite bank.

Please tell Catriona I'll be reunited with her soon. Her cryptic words on repeat in his mind, he dialed the sergeant's number.

It went straight to voice mail. Did that indicate the battery was dead? She wasn't in the mood to talk? Or had Bianca's warning come too late?

FIVE

This wasn't getting her anywhere. Cat had spent the last hour hunched over her laptop, scrolling through dozens of images. A majority were of Bianca at charity fundraisers. The candid shots of the young woman with her friends and boyfriend, Lane, revealed a more relaxed side. Cat had also scanned magazine articles. Public opinion was overall positive. The heiress had evaded scandal and appeared to use her wealth and position to effect good in the world. The biggest online controversy was over her decision to leave university after one year. While her naysayers said the move set a poor example, her supporters pointed to her grief as the reason. Cat couldn't relate on a personal level, having never known a mother's love. But Bianca had, and she'd lost it.

A new photo popped up, this one a close shot of the Winthrop head of security in action. Gray was more intense and focused in this setting. He appeared to be in complete control of the situation. There was zero hint of vulnerability. Of course, she'd met him in his worst moment, the aftermath being that he couldn't remember anything about his life.

Cat sat back in her chair and absently rubbed the sudden twinge in her chest. Surely she wasn't sad about saying goodbye to him?

At the unexpected crunch of tires on gravel outside, she left the table and crossed to the windows. Sometimes pizza delivery guys used her driveway as a turnaround spot. Anticipation tripped through her. Maybe Gray had decided to update her in person. Peering through the blinds, she saw an older black sedan with tinted windows. The driver exited the car and cast a furtive glance around.

Prickles of unease crawled up her spine. Her feeling that he wasn't there to sell her a vacuum was confirmed when he produced a Beretta.

Cat raced to her bedroom, dived into the closet and punched in the safe code. She removed her Glock and flipped the safety. Her only option was to use the rear exit and escape through the wooded area linking this property with her neighbor's. Once there, she could get out an emergency call.

Cat couldn't hear any other sounds above her heart's thundering warning thrum. She tiptoed through the room and paused on the threshold. On her left, the wooden plank creaked. She stepped into the hall and pivoted, with her gun raised. A man slammed into her, knocking her to the floor.

The air whooshed from her lungs. She worked to ignore her fear and maintain her cool. Gripping her weapon, she shifted onto her back and aimed. He kicked it from her grasp, reached down and seized a fistful of her hair. She cried out as he hauled her up and shoved her into the living room.

Cat fell against a side table. Spying her gun lying against the opposite baseboard, she lunged.

A heavy boot came down on her back, crushing her facedown on the throw rug.

"If you want to keep your half sister safe," he boomed, "you'll stop resisting."

She registered his words and the various throbbing points in her body at the same time. "You've got the wrong woman," she said, panting. "I don't have family."

Her gaze fastened on her gun, she curled her fingers into fists and tried to think of a way out. "I haven't seen your face. You can leave without fearing retribution."

The kitchen door opened and closed. Boots scraped along the painted boards. Pinned on her stomach, she could only make out dusty jeans and cowboy boots.

"What's taking so long?"

"She's a scrappy one," he defended, the boot digging deeper into her middle back.

She gritted her teeth.

"She's military," the newcomer said by way of explanation. "Let's go."

The man pointing a gun at her removed his boot, clamped his hand onto her upper arm and forced her to stand.

"I don't know who you think I am, but you've got the wrong person."

"You look enough like a Winthrop to convince me."

Stunned by the implications, she didn't struggle as the men marched her out the back and around the side to where their sedan was parked. A Winthrop? Her?

The man with the cowboy boots was younger and shaved bald. He opened the rear door.

She dragged her feet. "You've made a mistake."

"Get in."

The shaggy-haired man hustled her inside and dropped onto the seat beside her. She was very conscious of the gun barrel lodged between two ribs. One false move, and he could pull the trigger. The door slamming shut jarred her out of the whirlpool their claims had created. She was now trapped inside a vehicle with men who meant her harm. Allowing that had been a huge mistake. As a military law enforcement officer, she knew her chances of survival had dropped significantly.

God, it's me, Cat. I need You.

The bald one got behind the wheel and started the engine. The last fingers of sunlight allowed her enough visibility to catalog details of his appearance. She chanced a glance at the man beside her, and he responded by digging the gun deeper into her flesh.

Cat flinched and looked away. *Think, Catriona. Look for makeshift weapons.*

The pockets affixed to the seats were empty, as were the bench seat and footwells.

The car reversed toward the road, the tires gripping uneven gravel. Once they reached the main road and picked up speed, she'd have scant options left. She had to act now.

Adrenaline coursed through her. She would have to call on every hour of training the Marine Corps had provided. They were armed, so it was a risk. A huge one. But allowing them to take her to their hideout was the greater danger.

She closed her eyes and envisioned her plan.

"Watch out!"

A sudden jolt rocked the car to a stop. Her body jerked against the seat.

Curses assaulted her ears. "He's blocking you on purpose!"

Through the rear window, she could see an SUV rammed against their bumper. She recognized the driver at once. Gray.

"Drive through the yard," the shaggy-haired

man barked. Focused on the new threat, he lowered the gun.

The driver jammed the gear into Drive and circled in front of her porch. The car rocked and dipped.

Cat eyed the gun. All she needed was thirty seconds, maybe a minute, to throw open the door and jump out. How not to get shot in the process?

He pressed the gas. The mailbox got closer.

She was almost out of time.

Gulping in a breath, she elbowed the shaggy-haired man in the nose. He didn't see it coming. Blood spurted. An enraged growl exploded from him. She lunged for the door and grabbed the handle. Locked.

The driver hit the brakes, throwing her off balance.

"Come back here," the goon beside her yelled, spewing awful names.

He grabbed her hair again, yanking so hard her eyes watered. Cat felt herself falling backward. She would've landed on him if she hadn't grabbed the headrest.

Have to reach the lock—

"He's coming at us again," the driver alerted his partner. "Gonna try and cut us off."

"Gun it!"

The engine responded, and they hit the road's uneven edge too fast. The rocking motion slammed her captor against the opposite door.

Cat finally flipped the lock and shoved open the door. Grass and sandy dirt churned beneath her.

"No!"

She launched herself as far as she could and prayed she wouldn't fall beneath the spinning tires.

The struggle in the back seat played out before Gray's eyes. His heart went into jackhammer mode, and his veins sizzled with dread and fury. When Gray saw the car door snap open, a protest formed on his lips. She couldn't hear him. Probably wouldn't heed his warning if she could. "God, please protect her—"

Catriona hit the ground. He cringed. Would the thugs abandon their bid to abduct her and decide to end her instead?

She rolled clear of the tires. Gray swerved to the right and positioned the SUV between her and the sedan, which was gunning for escape.

He rushed to her side and helped her to stand. "Can you walk?"

Nodding, she eased away from him and began limping toward the porch. "Are they gone?"

"For the moment."

Once inside, he locked the doors and tested the windows. Catriona went straight to a side table and retrieved her weapon from beneath it. Her movements were cautious and stiff.

"Are you experiencing any light-headedness? Extreme pain or nausea?"

She laid it on the ancient dining table. "No."

"You're as white as a sheet," he informed her. "I'm trying to come to terms with the fact you jumped out of a moving vehicle."

"It was either that or give in to their plans for me."

Looking angry rather than rattled, she painstakingly removed several hairpins and let her hair fall loose about her shoulders. Then she ran her fingers through the thick mass, her discomfort obvious.

"Did you hit your head in the fall?"

"Let's just say if I see those two again, I'm going to teach them some manners." Her eyes smoldered with defiance.

"Catriona, how long were you alone with them?"

She lowered her hands to her sides. "Maybe five minutes. They didn't hurt me."

Relief eased some of the tightness in his chest.

"Walk me through what happened," he said, taking up position at the front door.

"I was on my computer when an unfamiliar car parked outside. The first man to emerge was armed. He entered through the back door while I was retrieving my gun. He ambushed me." Taking out a sheet of paper, she sank into a chair. "I need to record the details while they're fresh."

"I'll call in the license plate." He called the station and requested the information be passed to Detective Pike. "They're sending a unit over. I'll have to notify the rental company of the accident, but that can wait. If I had my weapon, I could've shot out their tires and prevented them from escaping."

The Jacksonville PD probably wouldn't be quick to return it. He was an unknown player.

She set the pen aside and shifted to face him. "How is it that you showed up at exactly the right time?"

"Simple. Bianca called and warned me."

"What?" She stood up too quickly and had to use the table to brace herself.

Gray left his post and crossed the room in four strides.

"I'm fine." Gaze on her tennis shoes, she put up a hand to ward him off. "The dizziness will pass."

Gray fisted his hands to keep from reaching out. The memory of her thoughtfulness in his hospital room was fresh in his mind, and he wanted to return the kindness. Since she wasn't receptive to him helping her resume her seat, he went into the kitchen and inventoried the fridge contents.

"What are you doing?" She appeared in the doorway.

"What do you prefer? Green tea or lemonade?"

"I can serve myself, Mr. Michaelson."

He noticed she let the jamb support her weight. Her freckles stood in stark contrast to her milk-white skin, and her pupils were dilated. A dark bruise was forming along her jawline.

"Don't you think it's time to drop the formalities?" He extended both bottles to her. She chose the tea but didn't open it.

"I'm not used to being waited on. Nor do I allow strange men to make themselves at home."

"We don't know yet if I'm strange or not. I could be a very boring person."

She arched a challenging brow at him. Twisting open the bottle cap, she tossed it in the trash can and returned to the living room. She didn't sit, even though she had to be sore. Instead, she went to the door and surveyed the yard and road.

"How was Bianca able to call you?"

"She bribed one of the guards and pretended to call her boyfriend, Lane." He waited for her to turn and look at him.

"Why would she do that?"

"To deliver a warning. She said to tell you that you would be reunited with her soon. Apparently, the person she was asking about the first time we spoke was you."

Something flickered in her eyes. "I see."

"You don't act surprised."

"Those thugs were acting under the assumption that I'm related to Bianca. They believe I'm her half sister, which is ludicrous."

Gray stared at her. "Has there ever been a public claim of another Winthrop child?"

"Not that I recall."

"If you were a long-lost Winthrop heiress, they could double the ransom amount."

"But I'm not. They're clearly wrong."

"The important thing is that *they* think you're valuable, which means you have a target on your back."

SIX

"There's no evidence," Cat contended, confused as to how she was suddenly a hot commodity.

Gray placed his hands on his hips. He tilted his head and scrutinized her more closely.

Her face warmed. "You're staring."

"You're both redheads."

"Bianca is blonde."

"Strawberry blonde. And she gets highlights."

"She does?"

His eyes widened. "I don't know how I know that."

"As the person in charge of her security, you'd be acquainted with her schedule."

Cat watched him digest the tidbit, watched the wonder fade when nothing else materialized.

His gaze cleared and refocused on her. "How old are you?"

"Twenty-four."

"Do you have a younger photo of yourself?"

"This is ridiculous," she said.

"Is it? How else do you explain our presence in North Carolina? At the park?" He gestured behind him. "Not just *at* the park, but in the one spot with a clear view of your home?"

She sank onto the couch, propped her elbows on her knees and kneaded her forehead. Her muscles, joints and bones ached from the brutal jarring the hard earth had given. Allowing even a glimmer of hope to exist was dangerous. After years of yearning, of daydreaming about a fictional family, she'd finally accepted reality. There wouldn't be a joyous reunion for her. She'd been abandoned, plain and simple.

She felt the cushions sag. "I know this is a lot to process. Your peace has been blown to bits in the past twenty-four hours."

She lifted her head. "I'm not a long-lost heiress. I was discarded on a social worker's doorstep as an infant. I was wearing a yellow-and-white polka-dot dress and white socks. A handmade blanket was wrapped around me, and there was a note with my name on it. Catriona. No middle name. No last name. No clues. Believe me, I've searched. There's nothing to find."

"Have you wondered why you were left with a social worker and not at a hospital or other safe place? Was this person known to your parents or guardian? Was she paid to keep quiet?"

"I don't know. I wasn't able to make contact with her."

"We don't have physical evidence linking you to the Winthrops. But we should at least consider the possibility."

At the arrival of a car in the driveway, they both hurried to the door. Pike exited the unmarked car, and a second unit parked on the road. The pair circled the battered rental car parked at an odd angle in the yard, then climbed the steps onto the long, narrow porch where Cat and Gray waited to relay what happened.

"I wrote down every detail I could remember."

Cat retrieved the paper, and the detective and officer skimmed the list together.

"The man who held you at gunpoint was thirty-ish, with shaggy dark hair, brown eyes and a thin nose." Pike regarded Cat from behind those thick lenses. "Any identifying marks or piercings?"

"I didn't get a good look at him. The bald one had a scar along one side of his neck," she said, running her finger along hers. "It was thin, jagged and white."

"Can you positively say these are the same men who attacked Miss Winthrop and Mr. Michaelson?"

"It was dark, and they stuck to the shadows."

"Mr. Michaelson, do you have anything more to add?"

"I was inside the vehicle the whole time."

Pike handed the paper to the officer, who returned to his cruiser. "Your timing was impeccable," she told Gray.

"Bianca took a huge risk," he said. "Have you unearthed any promising leads?"

"While she is active on social media, there isn't as much personal content as you might expect. She keeps the focus on her volunteer organizations and urges her followers to get involved in their communities. We have spoken to her boyfriend, and he's claiming he had no knowledge of this trip."

"Do any of Winthrop's business associates have reason to be involved?" Cat asked.

"We have no answers on that front. Mr. Winthrop isn't new to scrutiny. He's had a lifetime to install layers of privacy around himself and his company."

"He isn't willing to cooperate? His daughter's life is on the line."

"He's willing to a point." Her lips pursed in disapproval. "Do you have any theories as to why the abductors have turned their attention to you?"

"They claim I'm Bianca's half sister." The words sounded like a tabloid article. Everyone in the greater Chicago area was aware of the Winthrop dynasty and their decades of philanthropy. "I have no known relatives. I can assure you these claims are false."

Pike's curls bobbed as she tilted her head this way and that, piercing Cat with her owl stare.

"And yet they acted on the tip." She typed something into her phone. Reaching into her back pocket, she produced a leather wallet. "Mr. Michaelson, I believe you've been impatiently waiting for this."

Gray's expression was tough to read as he accepted the item. "Thank you."

"We've put a BOLO out for the car," Pike said. "Do you have an alarm system on the house?"

She shook her head. "My landlord doesn't see the need for one."

"I advise you not to stay here alone."

"I'll stay with her."

Cat jerked her head in his direction. "Excuse me?"

Pike held up her hands. "I'll leave you two to hash it out. Let me know what you decide. The department might agree to lend you officer presence for one night."

Gray waited until she was out of earshot before turning to face Cat. His chin was set at a stubborn angle. "I noticed a storage unit in the backyard. I can bed down in there. If you'd rather have me closer, the screened-in porch will do."

From a tactical standpoint, having a second person around made sense. Her personal choice was a solid no. "I met you twenty-four hours ago. What makes you think I'd let you stay on this property?"

"Like it or not, Catriona, we're in this together."

Her full name uttered in his deep, cultured voice threatened to melt her resistance. That irked her. Sure, he had serious, striking blue eyes that tested her defenses. Unlike the jarheads she worked with, Gray had thick, glossy hair that tumbled onto his forehead and begged for her fingers to smooth it. He had broad shoulders that invited her to rest her head and release her cares. Cat didn't welcome the way her senses became heightened when he was near. She didn't welcome the sudden craving for companionship and—dare she admit it—romance. A romantic relationship required more than she was willing to give. It meant being open and vulnerable, something she worked to avoid.

"We're both seeking answers." He took a step closer. "We'll get farther faster if we work together."

Cat mulled over her options. Changing her routine by sleeping in an area hotel might get noticed by someone in her unit. She couldn't afford for her current predicament to become common knowledge. Even a hint of scandal could tarnish her reputation and hinder her chances of advancement.

"The shed or the porch. It's your choice. For one night only."

Gray's wallet lay untouched on the table between him and Catriona.

"Are you sure you don't want some privacy?"

she said. Seated opposite him, she was unnaturally still. Her hands were folded in her lap, her posture military straight and her eyes watchful. After Pike had left, she'd disappeared behind her locked bedroom door and returned wearing clean clothes. The particular shade of her green shirt made her eyes shine. Her hair had been washed and combed into a sleek red curtain.

"Positive."

He wasn't entirely comfortable, either. He'd been prepared to argue his way to watching over her tonight, whether it be from the shed, porch or rental car. But protecting Catriona wasn't his only motivation, and that was the trouble. Bottom line—he didn't want to explore his past alone. The sergeant had proved to be courageous and resourceful. She'd be a suitable ally against Bianca's abductors.

A timer sounded in the kitchen behind her. "Pizza's done."

She left him alone again. He heard the oven door creak open, the pan slide against the rack and the door suction closed. His stomach growled in response to the aroma of golden crust, tomato sauce and melted cheese.

"Do you need help?" he called, his focus on the wallet.

"I'm good." She returned with twin plates bearing piping-hot slices. "This doesn't compare to homemade, much less Chicago-style pies. I'd planned to do the weekly grocery run tomorrow." Dashing back into the kitchen, she got grated Parmesan, napkins and drinks. "I guess you don't remember what kind you like."

"Could be a good thing. Maybe I'll discover I prefer nutrient-dense foods."

"Everybody has a weakness for junk food," she countered. "Kurt's was corn dogs."

"Kurt?"

"My fourth foster dad." Her lashes swept down, and she took her time chewing. "He was a youth pastor at a small church in the suburbs. He was the best."

"What happened?"

"He died of a heart attack."

"I'm sorry."

"I begged to stay with Dana and the kids. She wanted to keep me, but then she decided to move to another state to live with her mom." Frowning, she reached for her soda. "I don't know why I'm telling you this."

He'd noticed something was different about Catriona's home. The furnishings were well loved, eclectic pieces he guessed were thrift store finds. The patterned pillows, throws and rugs had been paired together with an eye to creating a restful haven. It wasn't the decor, he realized. It was the lack of personal photographs.

"Did you keep in touch?"

"She sent letters for about a year." Wiping

her fingers on the napkin, she tapped the wallet. "How long are you going to wait? The suspense is killing me."

Gray pushed aside his plate. "Let's hope this is more helpful than my phone was."

The first thing he found was a library card. Catriona's eyes brightened. Examining it evoked her first real smile.

"I'm impressed."

"Maybe I don't use it to check out books."

"You could be a chess club member."

"Or a car magazine fanatic." He pulled out three store loyalty cards. "I don't remember shopping at any of these places."

"Shopping isn't all that memorable, in my opinion," she said, scrunching up her nose. Pointing to a green one, she said, "This is a popular organic grocery store chain. Maybe you are health conscious."

"Or I went there once and the cashier insisted I get a loyalty card." Gray counted out ten twenty-dollar bills. "I can repay the nurses."

A shrewd look stole over her face. "Trust me, they were happy to donate to your cause. Is there an insurance card? Gym membership?"

Gray checked the remaining slots. "I missed one."

He stared at the black-and-white photo of himself against a blue background. The words *Armed Forces of the United States* jumped out at him.

"That's a DD Form 2." Catriona scooted her chair around to his side. "The blue color means you're either retired or on temporary or permanent disability. You're not old enough to have served twenty years. Maybe it's connected to your knee injury."

He was, or rather had been, military. Gray sat a little straighter, satisfaction filling him. "I wonder what MOS I had."

Catriona blinked at his use of the acronym for Military Occupational Specialty. As she studied him, her silver-green gaze clouded over. "You should return to the hospital and have them use the Social Security number listed here to dig into your medical history. This isn't your home state, but many clinics and hospitals have patient portals."

"I'm good."

Her gaze narrowed.

"Not one hundred percent," he amended. "But decent, considering."

"Considering you spent the night in the ER, you mean?" She made a dismissive sound. "What if you have a heart condition? What if you're supposed to be taking prescription medicine?"

"Pike would've told me if they'd found something to that effect in the SUV at the park."

"Would she?"

"I would know if my heart wasn't working right." It did react oddly whenever she was nearby. Not that he would ever utter something so trite.

Her lips pursed. "You left the hospital too soon."

He didn't have an argument for that.

She leaned over and grasped his wrist. "What's behind the zipper part of the wallet?"

Her touch distracted him. Her fingers were warm, her nails short with a clear sheen. A simple silver ring adorned her right hand.

Noticing his hesitation, she pulled away. He inspected the hidden opening. "Got something."

He removed a thick, folded paper and, laying it on the table, smoothed it open. Catriona gasped. She snatched it from his grasp, her brows snapping together.

"Why do you have a picture of me in your wallet?"

SEVEN

It was clearly a surveillance photo. Someone had followed her—stalked her—and snapped a picture without her knowledge or consent. Her throat itched with outrage.

Gray pushed back his chair and gained his feet. "I know how this looks—"

"Yeah, creepy." Cat deftly grabbed her Glock and tucked it in her rear waistband. She tapped the image of herself in conversation with her friends Olivia and Brady Johnson. "This was taken outside the church I attend."

"Listen to me—"

"You invaded my privacy. You were surveilling my home from the town park."

Cat mentally worked through the implications, acknowledging that she wanted Gray to be a good guy. But what she wanted didn't factor in. If her law enforcement experience had taught her anything, it was that human nature was wily and unpredictable. Some people were skilled at hiding their true selves. She had to consider Gray's amnesia might be a facade. He could be working with Bianca's captors. Perhaps they wanted something from her and figured inserting Gray into her life was the way to get it.

"I am not the enemy, Catriona."

She refocused on him, noting his relaxed stance and open expression.

"Think through the events. I showed up to warn you, not help those guys whisk you away."

"That's not sufficient evidence," she said, without much conviction. The shock of discovering the photograph was gradually fading. "You could be working a different angle, trying to ingratiate yourself into my life."

His brows winged up. "Allowing myself to be injured in the process is a little extreme, don't you think?"

"Everyone's definition of *extreme* is different. If someone is desperate enough…"

She stared at the photo and thought of the times she'd been duped. Fooled into thinking the popular girls liked her, when they'd really been angling to get close to the older teen boy in her foster home. Tricked into thinking Jared Lonas actually wanted to be her date to spring formal, when he'd simply been playing a joke on the poor, unwanted foster girl. Life experience had taught her to be cautious. Military brotherhood, the bond that developed between marines who worked and trained together, had provided a false sense of security, setting her up for the biggest mistake of her career. She'd thought Sergeant Toby Craft was like most other marines—honorable and trustworthy.

Gray's patient voice broke into her thoughts. "During the first phone call, you heard Bianca ask if I'd seen someone. A female, remember? Tonight she called to warn me you were in danger. She had to have confessed to her captors that you are her half sister, no doubt due to threats against her or her father. Catriona, you are the reason Bianca and I came to North Carolina. Whether or not her claims are valid, *you* brought us here."

High beams flashed across the front of the house, drawing them both to the windows.

"What is Olivia doing here?" This was far from an opportune time to visit.

"Do you want me to wait on the screened-in porch?"

Cat studied his profile long enough that he turned and met her gaze head-on. Her instincts said he was safe. Plus, she was armed, and he wasn't.

The knock was swift and succinct.

"She's already seen the rental car. It'll be easier to introduce you."

"What are you going to tell her?"

"No idea."

Unbolting the lock and swinging open the door,

she plastered on a smile and greeted her closest friend. Olivia was a hugger. Cat masked her discomfort—she was sure to be covered in bruises tomorrow—and accepted the thick workbook Olivia held aloft.

"They handed out the new Bible study books Wednesday night, and I promised Jody I'd drop it off."

"Thanks. I appreciate it." Cat hadn't participated in a women's study before and was slightly apprehensive about the prospect. Olivia had reassured her that sharing her private thoughts wasn't mandatory. "You just got off work?"

"One of our manta rays is ill, and we had to quarantine her. I'm hoping it won't take long to diagnose the problem." Olivia worked at the local aquarium. She gestured over her shoulder. "What's that vehicle doing in your yard?"

To their left, Gray shifted his stance, and the contrary floor beneath his shoes creaked. Olivia jerked toward the sound, her thick black braid slipping over her shoulder and jade earrings swinging widely.

"Hello," she ventured, curiosity peppering her voice.

"I apologize for startling you. The name's Gray Michaelson," he supplied, offering his hand.

"Olivia Johnson. Is that your vehicle?"

"Not exactly." His sudden smile was disarming, and Cat's tongue felt glued to the roof of her mouth.

Olivia's bright gaze bobbed between them. "Whose is it, exactly?"

"A rental. Gray is passing through the area." Cat finally found her voice. "He required some assistance, and I was in the right place at the right time."

Gray coughed and averted his gaze. A crease formed between her friend's brows, and she opened her mouth to speak.

Cat dropped the workbook onto the coffee table and took hold of Olivia's elbow, steering her toward the door. "Is Brady waiting at home for you? I suppose you guys have a nice dinner planned at Sullivan's." The Sneads Ferry restaurant was popular with the locals and base residents alike. "Are you still craving lime-flavored foods?"

"Actually, he's on a night flight. I'm in no hurry to get home."

Gray lifted his hand in farewell. "Nice to meet you."

Cat ushered Olivia onto the porch and shut the door firmly behind her.

"What was that about?" she demanded. "What aren't you telling me?"

"Trust me, you don't want to know."

"Oh, I think I do."

"It's complicated."

What an understatement. She could have an

heiress sibling who was being held for ransom. She was now wanted by the same abductors, and she was stuck with a mystery man.

Olivia framed her waist with her hands and leveled an obstinate stare at her. "I'm no stranger to complications."

Catriona had had a first-row seat to said complications. The widow's past had collided with the present in a spectacular way. Olivia had been living on the New River Air Station, the smaller base a few miles from Camp Lejeune, and Cat had been assigned to stand guard outside her house. Olivia often said God had used circumstances to orchestrate their friendship. The notion was a nice one, although it was difficult for Cat to believe He'd care whether she had friends or not. He hadn't cared that she'd grown up without parents.

"You have a little one to think about now."

"Being pregnant doesn't mean I can't be a supportive friend."

A lowrider truck with darkened windows rumbled past, music rattling the windows, and Cat tensed. She had to get Olivia away from the house.

"The truth is I'm intrigued by this guy. I'm enjoying talking with him," she blurted.

Olivia's hands slipped from her hips. "That's a first. You usually greet my matchmaking attempts with disdain." She tilted her head. "What's different about this one?"

Face smoldering like a burn pit, Cat tried not to squirm. This had to be convincing. "He's, ah, easy on the eyes."

"I can see the appeal," Olivia said wryly. "Older. Mysterious. Eyes that sweep you to a tropical paradise. He's a stranger, though. You're not immune to danger simply because you're military police."

"I can handle myself." She walked to the stairs' edge. "I'm not sure how much longer he'll linger."

"He didn't look eager to leave." A thoughtful expression flitted over Olivia's features. "Text me later."

Cat was tempted to confess what was really going on, but it was safer for Olivia if she kept it quiet.

"I will."

"I expect details, Cat." Patting her shoulder, she descended the stairs and navigated the tidy concrete squares connecting the porch to the driveway.

The light pole at the edge of the property winked on, a golden beacon in the bluish-pink haze. When Olivia had gone, she reentered the cottage and found Gray where she'd left him... at the window, with an unobstructed view of the porch.

"Spying on me?"

Sinking his hands in his pockets, he studied her with an unnerving gaze. "Watching out for you. It's not a good idea to be outside in the open. Those men could return at any time."

Cat sensed his reprimand had nothing to do with the threat and everything to do with her reservations about him.

"If my memory wasn't an issue, I could outline the events that led us to this point. I can't answer your questions. I can't explain why I was carrying your picture around in my wallet or how I obtained it. Maybe I took it. Or maybe I paid someone to." He lifted his chin. "I understand that I'm a risk, but there's a frightened girl out there who's depending on us. We have to work together to bring her home. I'm asking you to trust me, Catriona."

Gray had expected the silence that greeted his speech. He hadn't expected to be given the guest bedroom. Catriona's response had been diverted by a patrol car's arrival. Pike had made good on her promise. They would have Officer Wong's protection for the night.

"Here you go." Placing a pillow at the head of the twin bed, she said, "I haven't taken the time to hook up the television in the living room. Help yourself to whatever you find interesting on the bookshelf."

A painted aquamarine bookshelf held a variety

of books and magazines. "Have you lived here long?" he asked.

"About three months. I was in the barracks with other single lance corporals and corporals. Once I got promoted to sergeant, I was given the choice to live in town."

He imagined she'd jumped at the chance. "This is the first time you've lived alone?"

"Yes." She dodged his gaze. "If you get hungry, you know where the kitchen is."

"Thank you."

"Yeah, well, the shed is unsuitable for even a dog to sleep in. I also figured you wouldn't get any rest on the porch, and I need for you to be at the top of your game when the drop goes down tomorrow."

Pike had convinced Winthrop that the threat was indeed real, and he'd agreed to meet the abductors' demands. The money would be placed, as instructed, in a specific trash receptacle at the city park. JPD would be on site to identify the pickup man and follow him to Bianca's holding place. Catriona and Gray were too invested in the outcome to sit this out.

"Pike and the other officers won't be happy to see us."

"Then we'll make sure they don't."

EIGHT

"Are you sure this is the spot?"

Gray continued to observe the area around the specified garbage receptacle. "Positive." While at the station yesterday, he'd seen the map and heard the officers' description of the site.

"They're late," Catriona murmured, shifting restlessly on the bench. "It's five past the hour."

The city park was packed with people enjoying their day off. Kids ran through the splash pad situated between the target drop and the open-air pavilion where he and Catriona had stationed themselves. Parents watched over them from the benches situated around the pad, just out of the gushing fountains' reach.

The sound of a bat smacking a softball filtered above the trees, followed by cheers and whistles. A game was in full swing on the other side of the pines.

He stiffened when Catriona slung her arm around his shoulders and brought her face close to his. "Officer Wong emerged from the bathroom and is headed this way," she whispered, her watermelon-scented breath cooling his cheek.

From beneath his baseball hat's brim, he spied the plainclothes officer. If Wong recognized them, he'd boot them out of the park. Gray and Catriona trusted the authorities to do their best to rescue Bianca, but operations like these weren't perfect. He and Catriona would do anything they could to help bring her home.

Gray hooked his arm around her waist and, pulling her closer, angled his face toward hers. Her lips parted, drawing his gaze. They were well shaped. A few freckles had strayed there, barely visible against the dusky rose skin. Her freckles were charming, he decided, and softened the jaded toughness that characterized her interactions with the world.

The sticky, uncomfortable August heat was forgotten. He couldn't ignore how well she fit against him. Her shampoo smelled like the herb garden in his mother's sunroom.

He blinked as a vision entered his mind of a slim brunette bent over rows of plants.

"You went somewhere just now." Cat's fingers grazed his shoulder. "What did you remember?"

"My mom." He prayed she was still alive.

Her eyes reflected understanding. "Is Wong gone?"

Slowly shifting, he glimpsed the officer's back.

"He's circling around the playground."

Sighing, Catriona released him and, turning away, bent over the cheap umbrella stroller they'd picked up at the discount store. She moved the blanket aside to reveal a baby—a cute, round-cheeked doll that looked surprisingly lifelike. They'd chosen to disguise themselves as doting parents out for a Saturday stroll. Gray had donned a marine green T-shirt, camouflage shorts and sneakers. She wore a sleeveless navy blue blouse with tiny yellow flowers, and slacks. Her bright hair was hidden beneath a wide-brimmed sun hat.

"Why didn't they demand a wire transfer?" she asked. "Less risk of getting caught."

"Probably not savvy enough to avoid leaving a digital trail."

Because of his amnesia, he couldn't analyze the facts from his knowledge base. Were these people friends of Bianca's? Could they have perpetrated this prank at her request in order to claim Winthrop's attention? Was this a cry for help from an emotionally troubled woman? Arranging the drop at a busy public place could be the work of amateurs. Too easy for law enforcement to blend into the crowd and snag whoever picked up the money, or at least follow them in the hopes they'd lead the cops to Bianca.

"Got someone."

Catriona covered the doll and straightened, her shoulder bumping into his. "I see him."

A balloon popped nearby, and Gray jerked, instinctively knowing he didn't like loud noises. Didn't like crowds, for that matter. Catriona cut him a sideways look before refocusing on the man in question.

With a cell pressed to his ear and a disposable cup in the other hand, he paced back and forth beside the rectangular-shaped receptacle. On his periphery, Gray counted two undercover cops approaching.

The man appeared to be focused on his conversation. Was he a good actor? Stalling while he scoped out the crowd?

Walking closer to the garbage, he ended his call and glanced around.

Catriona stood. Gray caught her wrist. "Wait."

The next instant, an explosion rocked the ground beneath them. Screams shredded the air. Parents, their faces contorted in horror, stormed the splash pad, scooped up their children and ran for the parking lot. Officers drew their weapons and began to search for the source of the threat.

Gray left the bench and seized Catriona's hand. His first plan of action was to remove her from danger, until he followed her turbulent gaze to the large playground behind them and saw the wailing children. They were confused and terrified.

Together, they sprinted to the collection of slides and swings. They herded a group of four into the relative shelter provided by the largest structure. The stench of sweat mixed with hot metal and earthy mulch.

"I want my mommy!" A girl of about five cried, tears streaking down her cheeks and dripping off her chin.

Catriona sank to her knees and put a comforting arm around her. "It's better if we stay put, sweetheart. That way she can find us."

"Like in hide-and-seek?" she sniffled.

"That's right. What's your name?"

"Sarah."

"I'm not supposed to talk to strangers!" a towheaded boy shouted at Gray. "You're a stranger."

Sensing the kid was on the verge of bolting, he crouched in the low opening. "I'm Gray, and this is my friend Catriona."

"My friends call me Cat," she said.

"Gray and Cat. Those are funny names."

"I have a cat named Boo," the boy said in a calmer voice. "She's orange, like a pumpkin, and I got her on Halloween."

A third child pulled his thumb from his mouth. "That's a silly name."

"Is not."

"Is, too."

"Sarah!" A frantic woman appeared and held her arms wide. "You're okay!"

The girl launched into her mother's arms, who thanked them for their quick thinking.

"Paula!" She yelled and waved to someone beyond their view. "Leo's over here!"

They urged both women to remain with them until the all clear was given, but they were determined to reach their cars. As soon as the other two children were reunited with their guardians, Catriona left the safety of cover. Gray followed, not bothering to question her decision. With her law enforcement experience and his personal security background, they could be of help to more people. He was counting on his former training being instinctual.

They were passing the deserted swings when a second bomb detonated. The ensuing shock wave made his ears ring. Instinctively he hit the ground. Pain radiated through his knee.

The stench of metal and smoke filled his nostrils, and flashes of a war-torn desert assaulted him in rapid succession. He was rolling along in the Humvee, front passenger position. His buddy Karl was at the wheel. Two soldiers were in the back, one seated and one standing in the turret. Their vehicle was third in the procession. Theirs was the one to roll over the IED. The Humvee toppled and caved in on itself, the metal frame twisting around Gray and pinning him in. Couldn't open the door. Nothing but sand beneath his open window. And Karl… His friend had been killed instantly.

"Gray!"

They called his name, promising they'd get him out.

"Gray, can you hear me?" The feminine demand for attention snapped him out of the past.

Catriona yanked on his arm. "We have to move."

The chaos around him pushed in all at once. Sirens. Shouts.

He pushed off his knee, ignoring the throbbing ache. The nearest cry for help came from the stone path between thick stands of trees. The walkway led to the central parking area they'd passed on the drive in.

His mind didn't want to register what he was seeing. "It's Sarah."

The tiny child was lying prone on the ground. Her mother was bent over her in a protective position.

Catriona took off running.

No way was an innocent child going to die because of her. They should've anticipated this possibility. Should've cleared the park.

God, I need Your strength. Help me to help her.

Cat reached the mother and daughter and turned to speak to Gray. But he wasn't right behind her as she'd assumed. Scanning the terrible landscape of abandoned strollers and toys, she located him near the pavilion. He'd scooped an elderly woman from her wheelchair and, heed-ing the directions of a relative, was carrying her away from the park.

"Do you have medical training?" the mom demanded, pulling Cat's attention back. "Her leg's bleeding, and I don't know how to stop it."

"I'm not a professional," she said, explaining the basic knowledge MPs were taught. Cat inspected the wound—likely caused by exploding shrapnel embedded with the device—and asked for the mom's outer shirt. "We can use it to wrap the wound. The pressure will slow the bleeding, and the material will form a barrier against germs."

Tears leaking from her eyes, the woman removed the shirt.

"What's your name?" Cat asked as she worked.

"Gina." Smoothing Sarah's hair, she said, "Why isn't she awake? We were holding hands and running when the second one went off. The next thing I know, she—" A sob racked her. "I should've listened to your advice."

"Gina, listen to me. You were doing what mothers do—protecting their children."

With Sarah's leg tended, Cat debated whether or not to move her. It wasn't the best idea, but there could be more bombs. This narrow flagstone path was hemmed in by trees and profuse undergrowth on both sides—a blessing or a curse, depending on what it concealed.

Pounding footsteps and a tinny, whining sound

heralded the arrival of paramedics and a gurney. Cat stayed with Gina as the male and female duo simultaneously got a medical history and readied Sarah for transport. As they began to wheel the unconscious girl away, Cat's gaze probed the area for Gray. The trees blocked her view of the park's east side. He was likely still helping the older couple. She would've gone in search of him, but Gina looked as if she was on the verge of splitting at the seams. Cat had worked enough accidents to recognize the unspoken need. She would accompany the distraught mother as far as the ambulance, then double around and find Gray.

She kept pace with Gina, peppering her with questions that would distract her worst-case scenarios. Emerging into the grassy field adjacent to the parking lot, they came upon an active scene. A fire truck blocked one entrance. Police presence was immense. They would be working the scene already, on alert for the perpetrators, collecting witness statements and reassuring frightened citizens.

They wove through the maze of vehicles. The people they encountered had stunned expressions.

"Can you help me?" A man jogged over and addressed the paramedics. "My wife's having trouble breathing. I think she may be having a heart attack."

"I'm sorry, sir. We're on our way out." The female gestured to the general area. "Look for another medic or an officer."

The man's panicked gaze, barely visible beneath the forest green baseball cap, swerved to Cat, and she found herself offering to help. "Take me to her. I'll do what I can."

"Thank you, ma'am." He led her along the row of parked vehicles.

"How old is she?"

"Thirty-six," he replied.

"Does she have a history of heart problems?"

"No."

He circled around a group of people and, as they neared the row's end, lengthened his stride.

"What about panic attacks?" They could mimic a heart event. Cat prayed that was the issue.

"None that I know of." He stopped at a gray transit van and motioned for her to go ahead of him.

Cat skirted the front bumper, as it had been backed into the space, and searched the curb and thin strip of grass between the vehicle and the trees.

She noticed the side sliding door was ajar. No sign of the woman, but there was another man behind the wheel. A bald man with a jagged scar on his neck.

A gun was jammed into her ribs. "Do as I say, and no one else gets hurt."

NINE

Where was she?

"Thank you, sir." The gray-headed man pumped his hand. "You're a hero."

Anxious to find Catriona, Gray slipped his hand free and shut the trunk. The couple had begged him to return for the wheelchair, delaying his search. "You should go straight home," he gently instructed. "Your wife has had a shock."

"We both have." He waved at the park sadly. "We come here every day, you know, to enjoy the fresh air and reminisce about the times our kids played on that same jungle gym."

Gray wished he could spare the time to commiserate with them. He wished he could take them home himself.

As soon as the gentleman was ready to go, Gray halted the stream of traffic so he could back out. Finally, he could reunite with Catriona. He jogged along the deserted playground and found the flagstone path empty. On the other side, he encountered Detective Pike and Officer Wong.

"What are you doing here?" Pike barked at him, displeasure rippling around her. "Where's Sergeant Baker?"

"We got separated after the second explosion." He saw an ambulance leaving via the only open exit and wondered if she'd gone with Sarah and her mother to the hospital. "I'm going to look for her now."

"When you find her, both of you report to me."

Gray acknowledged the command with a nod. Sidestepping them, he entered the throng of authorities and civilians and searched for the flash of bright hair. She'd lost her hat somewhere between the pavilion and the slides, which would hopefully make his task easier.

Ten minutes later, he'd had no sighting of her and wasn't able to reach her on her cell. Something about this entire scenario was bugging him. The abductors had set up the drop site before learning of Catriona's existence. However, they could've changed plans in the intervening hours. They could've decided to abandon the payout— knowing they could double their asking price once they had both women in their grasp—and use explosions to distract and confuse law enforcement. He didn't know why he hadn't thought of it earlier.

Urgency gripped him, and he began uttering a silent, desperate plea to God.

When a gun report blasted through the crowd, pandemonium broke out. Gray ignored the shouts to get down and take cover. He had to get to Catriona in time. He couldn't let another woman in his life be taken against her will.

Cat struggled for control of the weapon. Her attacker was on the short side, but he was made of ropy muscles.

She kicked her leg, trying to hit him. He evaded her. Her hands were locked around his wrists, and he used that to his advantage, swinging her toward the van. She fell halfway into the opening. Unable to maintain her grip, she landed on her back. She brought her knees to her chest and kicked out, landing both feet against his chest.

He grunted and staggered back. The driver's door opened.

She couldn't fight two at once, especially not with innocent bystanders nearby. She had to run.

Bolting for the trees, she dived between the branches, cheeks stinging from the whip of pine needles. She tripped over a sawed-off trunk and went sprawling. The ground was unforgiving, and her sore body protested the hard contact. The air whooshed from her lungs.

Her pursuer crashed through the copse after her. Cat scuttled away, desperate to regain her footing. He clamped down on her ankle with a cry of triumph, anchoring her in place. He began to drag her backward.

Her fingers failed to grasp the passing trunks. Twigs dug into her thighs and stomach.

She twisted onto her back, forcing him to slow. She got a clear look at his face... Ordinary, even nondescript, other than the unrestrained greed in his eyes. He didn't see her as a human being. In his mind, she was the means to a life of luxury.

Cat jerked her leg with enough force to upset his stance, pulling him forward. She slammed his collarbone with her other heel. He instantly released her. She'd bought herself precious seconds. Sprinting through the trees, she emerged into another section of the park and ran between the tennis courts. Rounding the concrete building that housed the bathrooms, she paused to catch her breath and fire off a text to Gray.

I need you.

She was on the verge of telling him her location when, off to her right, the gray transit van entered her field of vision. Creeping along the side street. Looking for her. The bald guy looked right at her and spoke into a cell.

Change of plans. Cat bolted in the opposite direction, across the open field in the hopes of reaching the parks and recreation building on the far side of the park. Surely there would be park officials or police there. But first, she had to navigate more trees.

She was banking on these men wanting her unharmed. A dead hostage wasn't worth a dime.

At the tree line, she paused to look back and wished she hadn't. Her pursuer was fast. He'd pulled his gun again. He wouldn't shoot to kill, but he might shoot to slow her down.

Calling on her energy reserves, she burst through the trees and ran parallel to the softball field bleachers. While her typical MO was to navigate her personal affairs alone, she would've appreciated Gray's assistance right now. Then she recalled he wasn't armed. Her own weapon was locked away in her bedroom safe. A regrettable choice.

No one lingered near the softball field. Passing the snack bar, she glimpsed a trio of teenagers in uniforms. They looked at her with apprehension.

She skidded to a stop. "You have to leave. Now."

"We don't know which way to go."

"We got separated from our teammates."

"If another bomb goes off…"

Cat tried the snack bar door. Locked.

Frustration built. They were sitting ducks out here.

Wishing for her combat boots, she kicked at the knob multiple times and sighed with relief when it gave way. "Barricade yourselves in here." Pointing to the phone on the counter, she said, "Use the landline to summon police."

"Yes, ma'am." They shuffled inside, and she pulled the door closed.

"Gotcha." She was seized from behind, her arm wrenched behind her back until she thought it might snap in two. "Walk," he ordered.

When she started to struggle, he waved the gun before her face. "You don't want more casualties, do you?"

He must've seen the teenagers. Cat allowed him to propel her across the grass. The van jerked to a stop at the curb, and the side door slid open automatically. The shadowed interior loomed before her. They were going to succeed, she thought. These monsters would control what happened to her. Her stomach rolled.

The splintering of glass met their ears, and her captor spit out oaths that would make a marine blush. His fingers dug into her flesh. "Hurry up," he ordered.

His partner yelled for help.

Cat's confusion cleared when Gray came into view. He was wielding a baseball bat and using it to smash their windows to smithereens. The driver pulled a weapon. Gray ducked below the hood and, from the sound of it, turned his attention to the headlights. If they did manage to escape, the damage would make the vehicle easier to spot.

The warning blip of a police siren was music to Cat's ears. A patrol car turned the corner into the lot and the lights began flashing in earnest.

"Let's get out of here!" the driver shouted.

Cat was shoved to the ground. Her captor leaped into the space meant for her, and the van peeled away from the curb, almost clipping Gray. The engine revved as they completed a tight circle and zoomed through the exit onto the side street. Sirens blasted her eardrums. The chase was on.

"Catriona!" Gray raced over and laced his fingers with hers. His chest heaved, and his hair was in wild disarray. "You're okay?"

She shouldn't be *this* happy to see him. "I'm okay."

Together they took shelter in the parks and rec building. The entrance was unlocked, but there was no one inside. Gray propped the bat in the corner, locked the door and turned to her.

"Next time you text me," he said, his eyes a deep blue, "try not to be so cryptic."

"I got sidetracked."

"I noticed." Reaching out, he extracted several needles from her hair. Prickles rained over her scalp, and her breathing shortened. "Tell me what happened."

Cat was close to losing herself in his beautiful

eyes, to stepping into his arms and seeking comfort. She must be seriously addled to even think such a thing. She wasn't a leaner, wasn't a crier, wasn't a complainer. She was a tough, independent US marine.

"This was a setup. A way to get me alone so they could snatch me."

"They don't know I've lost my memories," he mused. "They counted on me being here. Considering I thwarted their attempt to take you before, they must think I've switched my protective detail to you."

"Meaning where you go, I go."

"Bingo."

"I hate to think how this second failure will affect Bianca." Would they take out their frustration on the young woman?

Gray texted Pike their location. He received an instant response. Stay where you are.

Not surprising, but Cat was anxious to get to the hospital and check on Sarah. Gray's phone came alive with an incoming video chat request.

Her heart climbed into her throat. The abductors with new demands or threats?

"Who is it?"

"I don't know." He flipped the phone to show her the screen.

"Dominick's Italian Eatery."

He swiped to accept the call. "Hello?"

"I'm seeing news reports of a bomb attack there. You heard anything about it?"

Gray's gaze bored into the screen. "It's a developing situation."

"There's something you're not telling me," the male caller accused. "Is it Bianca? What is that girl up to?"

Cat's breath hissed through her lips. No longer caring about respecting his privacy, she moved next to him.

"How do you know Bianca?" she said. "Better yet, how do you know Gray?"

The dark-haired man's eyes rounded. "Who are you?"

"Answer the lady's questions," Gray said. "Then we'll return the favor."

His jaw went slack. "Is this some sort of joke?"

"No joke." Gray's grim visage must've convinced the caller he was serious. "I haven't the slightest clue who you are."

"But—"

"I have amnesia."

Shock rippled across the caller's face. "How? What happened?"

"Your name and relationship to him first," Cat cut in.

"My name is Ryan. I—I'm your brother."

TEN

Brother? Gray located the nearest chair and lowered himself into it. Cat assumed the seat beside him and rested her hand on his arm. The warm connection kept him tethered to reality.

The man on the screen was a stranger. His face didn't jog a memory or evoke any emotion. "Why are you listed in my contacts as Dominick's Italian Eatery?"

"Because you're obsessed with maintaining a hard line between your personal and professional life. The fake names lend an extra layer of privacy. That's your business phone. You said that in the off chance it's lost or stolen, it would be tougher to connect you to your family members."

Made sense, especially considering the absence of social media trails.

"Are you going to tell me what happened?"

"Bianca's been abducted."

Ryan sank back in his chair and passed his

hand over his face. "You got hurt trying to prevent it?"

"I lost everything that makes me who I am." He checked the slide into self-pity and self-corrected. The other man hadn't been so fortunate. "Do you recognize the name Ross?"

"Ross Clark. He's part of your security team. Isn't he with you?"

"He died at the scene."

"I'm sorry, Gray. He was a good man." He sighed heavily. "You don't remember me at all?"

Catriona started to edge out of her seat. He missed her touch already.

"Hold on, Ryan." He held the phone to his chest. "Where are you going?"

"To give you privacy."

"What affects me affects you. We're in this together, remember?"

She almost looked ambivalent about that. In her career, she was obviously a team player. That was mandatory in military service. The time he'd spent with her revealed a level of distrust, however.

"You're sure?"

Nodding, he looked at Ryan again. "I should introduce you. This is Sergeant Catriona Baker. She witnessed the abduction and came to my aid. We're working together to bring Bianca home safely."

Catriona flashed Gray a grateful glance, which

he interpreted as gratitude for not sharing her stake in the situation.

"Thank you for helping my brother," Ryan said.

"You're in the position to help him, too."

"Right." His mouth quirked, hinting at mischievousness. "Painting a picture of Gray's life."

"Why do I suspect you're tempted to get creative with that?" he said.

Catriona nudged him. She'd pulled up a social media account belonging to Ryan Michaelson. Ryan obviously didn't share Gray's penchant for circumspection. His photos were set to public, allowing Catriona to scroll through them.

"Wait." He pointed at one in particular of Ryan and another young man at a football game. "There are *two* of you?"

A hearty chuckle bubbled up. "This is so weird, but fun, too. Yes, I have an identical twin. Fallon went air force after high school and has decided to be a lifer. He's stationed in Ramstein, Germany. I'm army, stationed in Fort Bragg, not that far from where you are."

Catriona chimed in. "You're twenty-two. Why the large age difference?"

Gray glanced over at her, trying to gauge her thoughts. She was referring to the twelve years separating him and his twin brothers. He was more interested in her attitude regarding the ten-year difference between him and her.

"Our parents had Gray within the first year of

marriage," Ryan supplied. "He caused them so much trouble they were dead set against having any more."

He uttered it with such conviction, his features open and honest, that it took them both a full minute to grasp his attempt at humor.

"Very funny," Gray mumbled.

He grinned. "I tell that to everyone who asks, and you have the same reaction every time. You need to lighten up, big brother."

"I'm guessing I hear that a lot."

"Yet you refuse to accept my wise advice."

"Any other siblings? How are our parents? Better yet, who are they?"

Ryan gave them a brief rundown of their family history. If his version was to be believed, they had a typical family life and shared a close bond.

"Am I involved with anyone?"

Ryan's gaze turned knowing. Catriona was suddenly distracted by a small rip in her shirt seam.

"You're married with five kids."

Catriona gasped.

"Ryan."

Another chuckle carried across the miles. "I see you haven't forgotten how to bark my name like a drill sergeant."

"Well?"

"Can't a guy tease his siblings once in a while?" Ryan held his hands up. "You were engaged to someone once. It didn't work out."

Gray's midsection settled somewhat. The news he'd been close to marrying was staggering. Those were details he would get later, when Catriona wasn't around.

"What can you tell me about my military service?"

The doorknob rattled, heralding the arrival of Pike and other officers.

Regret shuffled through him. "Shelve that for later," he said. "We have to go."

Ryan's expression turned serious. "When Mom sees the news report, she's going to want reassurances you're okay."

The image of the brunette tending her plants resurfaced. He would do his best not to ignore her attempts to reach him. "What did I file her info under?"

"Gloria's Greenhouse."

"Who's Gloria?"

"Our great-grandmother."

Pounding on the door was followed by Pike's irritated demands. Catriona went to let them in, and Gray disconnected the call.

The owl-eyed detective marched into the building. "You two have a lot of explaining to do, starting with why you infiltrated an active police operation."

"Can you remember any more details?" The sketch artist was hunched over his desk, his fingers darting over the page in a hummingbird pattern.

Cat fiddled with the paper coffee sleeve. The thin sleeveless blouse she wore offered scant protection from the frosty air blasting through the overhead vent. "That's everything."

They'd been at this for over an hour. After being castigated by Pike, they'd been ordered to the station to give an official accounting of every minute between their arrival at the park and their concealment in the parks and rec building.

"I'll input the specs into a specialized computer program later." He held up the oversize pad. "I like to do a paper sketch first. What do you think? Is this a close representation?"

She didn't have to study the likeness for long. "That's him. The driver." In the lower left-hand corner, he'd drawn an up-close view of his scar. "He was also at my house."

Swiveling to face his computer, he said, "I'll get this and the other drawing finalized before the eleven o'clock news."

Getting the suspects' information to the public quickly was vital in learning their identities. Combing through camera footage of the park and surrounding areas would eat up valuable time.

"Turn that up!"

Pike's bellow drew both Catriona and the artist out of the secluded office and into the bullpen where the officers worked. On a large television screen mounted to the wall, a news outlet was running an interview with Wayne Winthrop. It was clear he was in a foreign airport.

"While I've been conducting important business abroad, my daughter, Bianca, has been kidnapped," he stated, staring straight into the camera. "I have a message for those responsible—you will regret crossing me. If you hurt her, if you dare lay a finger on her, I will personally hunt you down and see that you pay, and pay dearly."

Pike threw her hands up and began to pace. "He was told *not* to leak this to the press."

Cat couldn't hear the reporter's question, but Wayne's disdain was obvious. "My sources have relayed the poor handling of my daughter's case by local law enforcement. I'm calling on the mayor of Jacksonville—no, the North Carolina state governor—to step in."

Pike skidded to a stop, fists opening and closing, her skin turning a mottled purple.

Gray returned from the evidence room. "What's going on?"

"Wayne has incurred the good detective's wrath," she murmured. She turned to the artist. "Am I done here?"

He nodded. "Escape while you can."

They walked in silence to the elevators. She punched the ground-floor button, and the doors swished shut. "I have a feeling Wayne Winthrop is going to be on the receiving end of a severe tongue-lashing." He cut an intimidating figure on screen, but he'd met his match in Marietta Pike. "Like many other powerful men, he does what he wants without thought to the consequences. I can't imagine what it must be like to work directly for him."

"I can't answer that." Leaning against the elevator wall, he scraped his hand along his jaw. Dirt streaked his shirt, and his sneakers were no longer pristine. His weariness was palpable. "I spoke with Ryan again while I was waiting to get my gun from Evidence. He informed me that I have a plan in place to leave Winthrop's employ."

"To do what? Protect another notable family?"

"Open my own security firm." The doors opened, and they emerged into the deserted lobby. "Whether anyone will be keen to hire me after this is debatable. I'm confident Winthrop doesn't give second chances, so I may be returning to Chicago in search of new employment. Housing, too. I live in an apartment on the grounds."

The reminder that he wasn't here permanently was a timely one. This situation was cocooning them into a false sense of connection. She hadn't known Gray Michaelson existed until two days ago.

As they passed the entrance desk, he spoke again. "Those things pale in comparison to the price Ross paid. The man lost his life. According to my brother, Ross left behind a wife and an adult son. Bianca is living her worst nightmare. She's staring death in the face, and she's got no one to comfort her."

Gray stopped and gingerly explored the stitches extending into his hairline. His fingers were trembling.

"What's wrong?" Alarm swept through her. Had the shock waves amplified his brain injury? "Are you in pain?"

"No." His gaze met hers. "I'm starting to have flashbacks. This one was of Bianca's mom's funeral last year. Bianca held it together throughout the service and the hours-long reception of friends and family at the mansion. Late into the night, the alarm for the pool gate woke me. I found her perched on the shallow end steps, still in her black outfit, the water up to her waist. She was hugging a picture frame to her chest and bawling her eyes out." His lips thinned, and he gave a short shake of his head. "Wayne should've been there to comfort her. Instead, the task was left to her bodyguard."

"I wonder if she and Lane were dating yet."

He shrugged. "I remember being angry at the injustice of it all. Bianca lost the one person who truly loved her. Tabitha's success was secondary to her daughter. Bianca was her number one priority."

This was more than just a paycheck. "You care about her."

"That's a fair assumption. I started working for the family four years ago, when she was sixteen. I was there through the tumultuous teenage years and the death of her mother."

After doing a quick survey of the parking lot and buildings on the opposite side of the two-lane street, they hurried to her car. Being out in the open made her antsy. The sun had sunk below the horizon, cloaking their surroundings in purple-edged shadows. Moths flitted around artificial light sources. The swell of cicadas warned summer was on its way out.

"I'd like to go to the hospital and check on Sarah." The explosions and the panic that ensued were fresh in her mind. How many others had gotten hurt? She jammed the key into the ignition, and the engine purred to life. "But I can't risk more innocent people's lives."

These men were determined to capture her, and they didn't care who else suffered.

Gray's lanky body crowded the hot rod's interior. He put his hand on her shoulder. "You're not responsible for the actions of criminals."

She stared out the windshield. "I've said those exact same words to victims over the years." She'd said it to herself before…in Okinawa. Those marines had chosen to steal from the US government, and she had chosen to report them. This felt different.

"Those bombs would've gone off whether you were there or not. They were taking a calculated risk."

"I forgot to thank you for coming to my aid. You're awfully handy with a baseball bat."

"Anytime."

His fingers tightened almost imperceptibly on her shoulder, his touch warm against her skin. She shivered as if she were in the sketch artist's office again, being blasted with cold air. In the dimness of the car's interior, their faces illuminated by the dash glow, his eyes were more black than blue. The moment stretched, heavy and expectant. Were either of them even breathing?

A car alarm jarred the night, and she jerked. His hand slid away, and he turned to stare out of the passenger-side window. She'd pay top dollar to know his thoughts. Better not to know, she decided. Romance wasn't on her agenda. Wedding bells and babies? Not in the near future. Maybe not ever. It wasn't like she'd know what to do with a husband and kids.

Her career was her life. And this mess she'd landed in posed a distinct threat to her professional plans.

Cat checked the rearview mirror every few minutes during the drive home. They arrived without incident, but her relief was short-lived.

"Someone's paid you a visit," Gray said, popping open the door and removing his weapon from his holster. "Any chance your landlord decided to drop in?"

"Unlikely." Her front door stood wide open. The light fixture beside the door was shattered into pieces. "He gave me the keys the day I moved in. I haven't seen him since."

Gray joined her, his expression tight. "We go in together, we come out together."

"You won't get an argument from me, seeing as I don't have a gun or a bat."

Together, they walked a diagonal path to the nearest corner and, hugging the house and staying low, climbed the stairs. Thanks to the old, warped boards, their arrival wouldn't go unnoticed. Glass crunched beneath their shoes. They waited, on opposite sides of the door frame, for several long minutes. Gray gave the nod and pivoted into the empty space, his gun outstretched. Cat followed in his wake.

If she'd been armed, they could've split up and completed the search in half the time. Her muscles were tight with trepidation, her pulse ramped up, her skin clammy. The day's events had rattled her.

Pretend this is a routine call. Forget the stakes are personal and focus on the task.

The spare bedroom to their immediate left was empty. Returning to the living room, they crept past the sofa and chairs and turned left into her bedroom, which was also clear. The lone bathroom wasn't harboring any intruders. That left the kitchen and screened-in porch.

Gray worked the cottage like a professional, his movements methodical and controlled. No one ambushed them in the kitchen. The back door scraped the porch floor as he nudged it wide, and a chorus of frog croaks serenaded them.

They edged into the space that offered little protection. A bullet could pierce the porch's flimsy screens and thin wood framework. Since she carried exchange value, she wasn't the target. Gray was the one they'd want to eliminate.

"Hand over your weapon and get behind me."

He immediately halted, and she bumped into his broad back. "You choose this moment to joke around?" he whispered.

"I'm not joking," she retorted with heat. "If anyone's getting shot at from those woods, it's you."

"I'm not trading places with you, Sergeant."

"But—"

"Shh." He slowly tilted his head toward the far corner.

Hearing a rustling sound, she stiffened. Metal rattled. A large ceramic owl toppled off its stand and crashed to bits.

Gray shifted toward the ruckus and shielded

her with his body. Cat recognized the blur of orange and white zigzagging in front of them.

"Don't shoot," she urged, gripping his waist. "That's Ziggy, the neighbor's monster cat."

The tension ebbed from him, and he lowered his gun. "How did it get in here?"

"He's resourceful. That's all I can say."

Stretching to push open the screen door, he held it open until the feline escaped. Then he sneezed. Multiple times.

If there had been anyone hiding in the woods awaiting their return, they would've already seized their chance.

They went inside and, after securing the doors, combed through the house for signs anything was missing. Her belongings hadn't been disturbed. They'd come for her.

Gray's expression was grim. "My guess is they had the explosives in place, but they came here on the off chance they could nab you and forgo the fireworks."

Cat surveyed her cozy nest of a home. She felt cheated. Violated.

She picked up the parrot-shaped dish that had been a gift from her foster mom Dana. Somehow it had survived several moves, including across the ocean, to Okinawa.

"I can't stay here."

But where could she go? Stacie Reid, her best friend in the Corps, was stationed in Camp Pendleton, California. Brady and Olivia would jump to offer her shelter, but she couldn't endanger them or their unborn child.

She was used to handling life on her own terms. Why seek God's help when she could take care of things herself? This situation was deteriorating fast, however. She wasn't sure which way to step, because so far, she'd been making the wrong moves. And one of these times, it might just get her and Gray killed.

ELEVEN

Gray hefted the bulging paper sacks onto the counters and pocketed the keys. Catriona wandered through the vacation rental home switching on lamps. Because of its waterfront location, the kitchen, dining and living areas were situated on the upper level. The bank of windows overlooking the intracoastal waterway boasted a black canvas sprinkled with flickering white lights.

Situated in a high-traffic area less than a mile from the sheriff's office, the home had been built on pillars. The yard was free of shrubbery and plants, and there was plenty of space between them and the neighbors. The commute from Swansboro to Jacksonville was under thirty minutes. Catriona would be reporting to work Monday morning, and she needed to remain within reasonable driving distance to the base.

He began to unload the sacks. "You want a sandwich? Yogurt? Brownies?"

The overhead light washed out her complexion

and emphasized the slight chafing on her cheeks she'd said was from her dash through the trees. She hugged her arms around her middle. If they were better acquainted, he'd offer the haven of his embrace. His gaze was drawn to her hair, a fiery river cascading to the middle of her back.

Snagging an apple before it rolled off the counter, she washed it in the sink. "I'll make do with this until morning. I don't have much of an appetite."

Neither did he, even though they'd skipped supper.

"I'm going downstairs," she said. "The hospital staff probably won't divulge information about Sarah, but they might give her mom a message for me."

"If you do talk to her mom, tell her I'm praying for her."

She looked startled. "You're a man of faith?"

"I can't remember the actual decision or the moment I became a follower of Jesus Christ. I do know I've memorized Scripture in the past, because sometimes verses spring to mind. Prayer feels natural and necessary. It's my link to God." He stowed the coffee creamer in the fridge. "What about you?"

"Kurt and Dana were active in their church, and when they went, I went. After months of hearing about this wonderful Father—a holy, perfect Father who would never abandon me—I decided I wanted a relationship with Him. Kurt prayed with me the night I put my faith in Jesus." A wistful smile curved her lips. In a flash, it was gone, replaced by a thoughtful frown.

"What's bothering you?"

"I'm realizing that I've failed to surrender all aspects of my life to God. It's easier to try and manage on my own. You know, the day-to-day stuff I assume He's uninterested in."

"It's natural to try and live life on our own terms," he agreed. "We just have to remind ourselves that He *is* interested and wants to guide us and give us strength."

"You're awfully wise for someone suffering from amnesia."

"Imagine what I could do with a fully functioning brain," he teased, winking at her.

Catriona smiled. Apple in hand, she descended the stairs. The fact she was a fellow believer comforted him. The fact he was intrigued by her had the opposite effect. He shouldn't want to discover what made her smile or what made her cry. He shouldn't have this pressing desire to know if she preferred walks in the rain or reading books by the fire, chocolate or vanilla ice cream, mountains or oceans, dogs or cats. He definitely shouldn't want to feel her hair trickling through his fingers.

They led very different lives in different parts of the country. While distance could be dealt with, the age gap couldn't. She was too young.

A full decade separated them. She would be more suited to one of his siblings.

His hold on the potato chip bag tightened, and it popped. Crispy disks scattered across the tile floor. Scowling, he went in search of a broom. Ryan and Fallon would never meet Catriona Baker.

Cat ascended the stairs late Sunday morning and was greeted with the sight of Gray in a full apron. On the massive kitchen island, he'd placed a coffee carafe, croissants and assorted jams.

"Did our mother teach us to cook?" He hadn't noticed her yet, as he was engaged in a video chat and had his back to her.

"You were the only child for years. Of course she taught you. We, on the other hand, got instructions on how to assemble sandwiches and make boxed mac and cheese." His brother's voice sounded from the screen.

Gray's laugh, rich and husky, warmed her to the soles of her feet. He'd changed into the other clothes he'd purchased—black pants and a heather-gray polo. The soft shirt pulled and gave with his movements, emphasizing his solid, uncompromising strength.

He pivoted and noticed her standing at the top of the stairs. His welcoming smile burned right through her with the force of the noonday sun. Cat reached for the stair railing, tempted to return to the cool isolation of her bedroom.

There's no room for cowardice in a marine's heart, she reminded herself. *He's no different from the other men you serve alongside.*

His gaze returned to the caller. "I've got to go. We'll talk later."

"Take care, big brother."

Gray slid the phone into his pocket, removed a mug from the cabinet and poured her a morning-sized coffee.

"How did you sleep?"

"Decent."

His gaze fell to where she held fast to the railing. "Did you forget something downstairs?"

"I'm trying to decide if that apron is a good fashion choice." Approaching the island, she slid onto one of the stools and accepted the coffee.

"It was the only choice," he quipped, his grin widening. Gathering dishes from the counter behind him, he set them before her. Boiled eggs, bacon and crepes.

"Crepes?" Was he for real?

He settled on the stool next to her. "Crepes were one of the first things my mom taught me."

"Ryan told you that?"

"Fallon." Snagging a croissant, he pulled off a flaky layer and popped it in his mouth.

"You trust your brothers to tell you the truth?" So it must have been Fallon on the video chat.

"I'll verify the boys' accounts with my mom."

"Boys?" She raised her brows. "I doubt they'd appreciate you calling them that."

Something flickered in his eyes, and his expression became careful. "They're much younger than me," he said lightly. "As are you."

Her cheeks warmed. The betraying pink was surely suffusing her face. Had he guessed she was affected by him? Did he think she had a crush? *Did* she have one?

"True," she agreed, busying herself with arranging berries on her crepe. "You're practically old enough to be my father."

Gray choked on his coffee, and she thumped him on the back. He held up a staying hand, irritability replacing his previous good humor. "That's taking it a bit too far, don't you think? I was barely ten when you were born."

Hiding a smile, she shrugged and forked a bite of the crepe. "What does it matter?"

"It doesn't," he muttered.

He lost himself in his breakfast, and Cat did the same. It was the best meal she'd had in days. When she'd had her fill, he slid his phone toward her.

"I couldn't sleep last night, so I did some digging into Wayne and Tabitha's past."

Cat scanned the old tabloid article. She remembered hearing rumblings of marital troubles. The claim that Tabitha had engaged in an affair was news to her, however. "I wonder if there's a shred of validity to this."

"If Tabitha had an affair during the years before Bianca came along, that's a potential link to you." He pointed to the screen. "There are more articles with similar tales. Wayne was reported to have been on the verge of divorcing her."

As a fan of Tabitha's music, she'd kept abreast of any news related to the star. Online sites tended to circulate the same photographs. This article contained one Cat hadn't seen before, one taken before Tabitha caught the music world's attention. She looked so much like her daughter. Rather, Bianca looked like her mother.

Cat searched for something of herself in Tabitha's features, hair and physique. Could it be possible? Could this talented, creative and successful woman be her mother?

"We will find answers."

They were both searching for keys to their past. "What if we don't like what we find?"

"We trust God will give us the strength to cope."

TWELVE

"What has you distracted today?"

Her shift partner, Winston Miller, tapped the steering wheel in time to the radio.

"Slow morning." Cat returned her phone to her cammies' outer pant pocket, 50 percent relieved and 50 percent worried Gray hadn't reached out. Had he been angry to wake and find her gone? In hindsight, her decision to call on Pike for a ride to work and slip out without his knowledge seemed immature.

"I'd rather be handing out speeding citations than dealing with domestic disputes," Miller said. "Remember that one on Tapalca Avenue?"

"How could I forget? You put yourself between an irate wife and a flying bowl and wound up wearing spaghetti and meatballs."

Flipping the turn signal, he huffed a breath of disgust. "Why people who don't like each other decide to get hitched is beyond me."

Gray had loved someone enough to propose

marriage. She didn't like the idea. She wasn't jealous of a stranger, of course. It simply wasn't fair that he couldn't remember a past relationship that had obviously been important to him. How recent was the breakup? she wondered.

Clenching her hand, she tried to absorb herself in the housing units and playgrounds rolling past her window. She'd spent all of Sunday in his company. There'd been no bullets flying and no abduction attempts…just her and him in this idyllic waterfront home. To her dismay, she'd enjoyed his company. Gray was witty and thoughtful. He was a good listener. He had a way of making her want to lower her guard and pour out the hurts and hard lessons she'd endured through the years.

That was why she'd slipped out this morning without waking him. Cat had felt suffocated. It had been a lousy thing to do, though, and she'd been on pins and needles ever since.

"You didn't answer my question, Baker. You've checked for messages at least once every quarter hour. You're more uptight than usual. What aren't you telling me?"

"You think I'm uptight?"

"You aren't going to tell me," Miller surmised. "No one can ever complain you're an oversharer."

"That's a good thing."

"Maybe. Maybe not." He shrugged. "Everyone is on edge after the bombings. I'd give my gun if the local PD would let me help search for the culprits."

A burning sensation spread behind her sternum, and it felt like guilt. "Our jurisdiction is contained to military installations and the immediate surrounding areas."

"I know," he said with a sigh. "And it stinks. At least there weren't any fatalities. I read that ten people were transported to the hospital. Six were treated and released, while the remaining four were listed in serious condition."

Cat had finally heard from Gina late last evening. Sarah was supposed to make a full recovery. During the conversation, Gina had repeatedly thanked her for helping her little girl. The mother's attitude would do a one-eighty if she knew Cat was responsible. The men and women in her unit would look at her differently, too.

Miller turned into the headquarters and guided the cruiser into a parking spot directly across from the main entrance. "Where are you going for lunch?"

"I thought I'd pick something up from the exchange."

His response was lost to her, because her gaze had homed in on two men conversing by the bike rack. One was in uniform, the other a civilian.

Her appetite fled. What was Gray doing here? And what was he doing with her immediate superior, Staff Sergeant Taube?

She exited the vehicle on wooden legs. It had slipped her mind that Gray had a retired military ID and could access the air station base. Absently bidding Miller goodbye, she approached the pair, silently pleading with God. *Please don't let Gray have said anything to Taube about my connection to the abduction and bombings.*

Taube was aware of her trouble in Okinawa. While he'd been aloof at first, he'd given her a chance to prove her worth. She'd worked hard each and every day, giving 110 percent and then some to earn his respect. Her success depended on maintaining a spotless reputation. Anything that called her skills or moral standing into question had the potential to undo her progress.

The staff sergeant noticed her approach and lifted a hand in acknowledgment. "Here's Sergeant Baker now."

Gray turned and inclined his head, his features inscrutable. The warmth she'd seen in his eyes yesterday had cooled considerably. "I've come to take you to lunch, Sergeant." He handed her the Chevelle keys.

"I see." Switching her attention to Taube, she said, "Did you need me for anything, sir?"

Her palms growing clammy, she scrutinized him for the slightest change in the way he regarded her.

"Nothing comes to mind," he said, his forehead bunching. "Go. Enjoy your lunch."

Without a word to Gray, she pivoted and marched toward her vehicle. He fell into step with her, followed her to the driver side and put his hand on her door to keep it from opening.

"What are you doing?" She cast a frantic look over her shoulder. Taube had gone back inside the building, but she didn't want anyone to witness this confrontation.

"Getting answers," he said quietly. A muscle ticked in his jaw.

"Not here, you aren't. This is my place of work."

"Fine."

Walking around to the other side, he dropped into the passenger seat and fastened his seat belt. Pulse bucking, Cat joined him inside the vehicle and was careful not to let their shoulders bump or forearms brush. Her keys dug into her palm. "Did you tell Taube how we met?"

"No. Why?"

"Did you mention that I'm connected to Jacksonville's recent rash of crimes?"

"I had a brief conversation with the man," he supplied. "As soon as I discovered you'd left, I came straight to the air station. The visitor center directed me here, where I was informed you were at the armory. I decided to pass the time until lunch at the personnel office. I—"

"Did you get your military records?"

"No. I'll have to contact the National Archives.

Fallon's already given me a brief rundown of my time in the Rangers and the IED that led to my medical retirement, but I'd like an official report." He tapped a slim cardboard box. "I also purchased a tablet. My laptop's at home, so I figured I'd use this while I'm here."

"When did you meet up with Taube?"

"Literally minutes before you arrived. He asked if he could direct me somewhere, and I told him I was waiting for you. That's it."

Her panic beginning to subside, she started the car and drove to the one stand-alone fast-food restaurant on the base. She parked in an outlying spot and, exiting the car, retreated to the welcome shade offered by an old, grand live oak.

"Why didn't you text me?" she threw out. "Why show up here?"

He shut his door with a quiet click. He walked to the front of the car, leaned against the wide hood and crossed his arms. His sharp gaze tracked her movements, questioning and challenging her. "Am I your prison guard and you my prisoner?"

"Excuse me?"

"Did you think I'd attempt to physically prevent you from leaving? Is that why you snuck out?"

"Of course not."

"Then why bother Pike when I was right there?"

Cat sagged against the tree trunk, deliberately not meeting his gaze. She couldn't tell him why.

When she didn't respond, he said, "I get that you'd rather be the lone wolf in this scenario, but we have to stick together."

Lone wolf? That was how he saw her? Catriona Baker against the world?

His assessment wasn't far off the mark. "I've had to depend on myself for most of my life."

"You can depend on me," he declared, his gaze holding hers captive.

She wanted to believe him. To trust him.

"Why did my talking to your superior upset you?"

A denial sprang to her lips, but she choked it down. "There was trouble at my last duty station. I was punished for reporting a crime, and it nearly ended my career."

"What happened?"

"I witnessed marines stealing weapons and ammo. When I reported it to my superior, he didn't quite have the reaction I was expecting."

"He was involved?"

Disillusionment swept over her features. "Sergeant Craft set out to discredit me, and he did a bang-up job of it, too. It's by the grace of God I wasn't discharged." The details she went on to reveal were difficult to hear.

"I'm sorry you had to endure that."

"I hate that they are probably still stealing from the Corps. I've had to claw my way out of the hole they put me in—professionally and personally. That's why I have to avoid even a whisper of trouble."

"Isn't there someone you can go to? An unbiased party who could look into it?"

"No." She pushed off the tree. "You have no idea what I went through. The social media backlash was horrifying, until I eventually became numb to it. I've rebuilt my career. In fact, I'm on the verge of being approved for special training. No way am I going to risk it all on the slim chance someone will believe my version of events."

Gray let the matter drop…for now. "Are you up for a road trip after work?"

She looked bewildered for a moment. "What sort of trip?"

"I found something," he said. "I used my new tablet to dig into Tabitha's history. That took me on several dead-end rabbit trails. However, I did learn that her close confidante, Hermione Allen, settled in Wilmington some years ago. I reached out via social media, and she's open to talking to us."

"I'm familiar with the name. Hermione's an accomplished painter. She used to hold exhibitions in and around Los Angeles. Most of her profits went to charity." Her eyes brightened. "Wayne has been a closed book regarding his late wife. I wonder if Hermione will be more forthcoming."

Wayne had vehemently denied the existence of another child. Gray's instincts said the man's protests were suspect. "Wilmington's only an hour drive from here, according to the map."

She nodded. "I've been to the downtown district many times."

"We'll be on our own," he felt compelled to warn. "The department doesn't have the manpower to provide an escort."

"This is important."

"I agree."

They would both be armed in case they were followed, which he would take every precaution against. After lunch Catriona returned to work, and he hung out at the exchange doing more amateur sleuthing.

Finally, they were zipping down Highway 17 toward Wilmington. Catriona kept a change of clothes in her car—it was against policy to wear the uniform in town—and had switched out her cammies for jeans and a dark, nondescript T-shirt. They reached the outskirts of the city without incident. Hermione lived in an upscale condominium complex located near a popular shopping area.

"There's a black SUV behind us," Catriona announced a mile from their destination, scowling into the rearview mirror. "We picked him up at the split four miles back."

Gray studied the suspicious vehicle using the side mirror. There were two men inside, but he couldn't make out their faces.

"No one followed us from Jacksonville." They'd traveled the four-lane highway that was a straight shot between the two cities. Traffic had been light, and there'd been nowhere to hide or blend in.

"I searched for tracking devices." The condominium entrance loomed, but she didn't apply the brakes. "I'm not going to take the turn. I'll continue along this road and make a U-turn."

"Get ready. They're coming alongside us." Gray reached for his gun.

The SUV whizzed past. The darkened windows prevented them from seeing inside. Catriona slowed the car, and the SUV turned into a gas station and parked at the pumps.

A long, ragged exhalation escaped her. "Looking for threats around every corner is exhausting." She pulled into a pharmacy parking lot, cruised around the building and reentered traffic. "I can't stop thinking about Bianca. She's in the lion's den, alone and helpless."

"They will keep her alive," he told her. "She's their gold at the end of the rainbow."

Catriona located the condominium number, parked and shut off the engine. Turning her head, she punched him with her gaze. "Keeping her alive and treating her well are two very different things."

The thoughts crowding his mind weren't pretty. In this instance, having amnesia was a blessing.

He was able to approach the case from a detached standpoint, to process facts without the distraction of emotions. Despite the short amount of time he'd spent with Catriona, he already knew he'd go out of his mind if she were to be taken.

Together they walked the short sidewalk to Hermione Allen's door. The doorbell pealed through the condo, and they heard her padding approach. The door opened, revealing a smartly dressed blonde in a flowing print dress.

When she glimpsed Catriona, she gasped and lifted a hand to cover her mouth.

Catriona shifted uncomfortably and glanced at Gray.

"Mrs. Allen?" he said. "I'm Gray Michaelson, and this is—"

"No need to say more," she interrupted, recovering. "You're Catriona, Tabitha's daughter."

THIRTEEN

"You're the spitting image of Tabitha. Oh, not in her post-fame years, not with those fancy hairstyles, highlights and high-dollar makeup. Her stylist did everything she could to erase the unpolished girl she once was." Hermione led them into the living room and thrust a faded photograph into Cat's hands. "I have a box of old photos in my office. After hearing from Mr. Michaelson, I pored through them and came across this one. The resemblance is uncanny, don't you agree?"

Cat stared at the color photograph of a young, smiling Tabitha, her fingers tightening on the rounded edges. Her head felt lighter than her body, and a hot flush swept through her. Awe mingled with her old enemy—hope. Hope that she wasn't alone in this world. Hope that, somewhere, she had a familial connection.

Gray crowded her space, his hand coming to rest on her lower back, supporting her. She didn't let herself lean into his steadying strength, but neither did she move away.

"You could be her twin in this photo," he murmured.

Cat couldn't speak. Was this all a coincidence? Or could she truly be the daughter of this accomplished, talented woman?

Gray cleared his throat. "Wayne denies the possibility that Tabitha had another child. The strong resemblance between her and Catriona calls his account into question. What can you tell us?"

Hermione suggested they sit. Cat welcomed the comfort of the sofa. Gray sat close beside her while Hermione took the opposite armchair.

"Tabitha loved Wayne, despite his complicated life. The happiness they enjoyed in the early years was marred by her inability to get pregnant. When she finally conceived, they were ecstatic. He was overjoyed at the prospect of welcoming an heir. Sadly, she miscarried, and the disappointment drove a wedge between them. He became distant and immersed himself in his work. Tabitha funneled her energy into building her music career. She met someone in the business, Anson Scott. They had a brief fling." She shook her head, her eyes glazed with past memories. "Tabitha felt terrible, so she ended things and confessed to Wayne. He was livid. When she learned she was pregnant, Wayne was determined to divorce her. His mother talked him out of it. Better to hide the child's existence and pretend it never happened."

"Why couldn't she have the baby and raise her as a Winthrop?" Gray interjected.

"Wayne's a prideful man. From birth, the mantle of Winthrop importance has been impressed upon him."

"Why didn't Tabitha fight for her child?" Cat asked, reliving the sting of abandonment.

"She was riddled with guilt. She allowed herself to be steamrolled by the Winthrop dynasty and ultimately agreed to give her baby up for adoption."

Gray wrapped his arm around her and cupped her shoulder, squeezing gently, attempting to infuse her with his warmth and strength. She didn't love that he was an eyewitness to her vulnerability. The lost, hurting little girl she'd been was clawing her way to the surface. Cat forced herself to meet his gaze. The blue depths didn't hold pity. They communicated friendship and caring. He'd said she could rely on him, and oh, how she longed to believe him. She was tired of depending solely on herself.

"Tabitha loved you." Hermione shifted forward in the chair. "She bought gifts for you, even knowing you would go to live with another family. I'm afraid I don't know where they ended up."

"We don't know for certain that I am her daughter."

"Something led Bianca to you," Gray stated.

"I won't believe it until I have scientific proof. Thank you for seeing us, Mrs. Allen. We won't take up any more of your time."

Hermione insisted she keep the photo. Then she hugged her. "When you find your proof, please come and visit again."

Cat let herself be enveloped in the older woman's arms, the same arms that had likely consoled Tabitha.

"We've got trouble," Gray warned from the window.

Cat slipped free and joined Gray. An old white passenger van with a terrible paint job was idling beside the fence-enclosed pool. She recognized the bald guy behind the wheel.

"How did they find us? We would've seen them if they'd followed us from Jacksonville."

"Maybe there was a tracker after all. Technology has gotten sophisticated. Easier to conceal these days." He told Hermione to call condo security. "That should divert them long enough for us to slip away. But we'll make sure they see us, so they don't come looking for us here."

To her credit, the woman didn't panic. She did as Gray instructed. "He's on his way."

"You should lock yourself in the bathroom and

call 911," Cat said. "Stay on the line with them until police arrive."

Cat didn't want another person to be hurt, especially Hermione. She was a vital link to the woman who might be her mother.

"Take my car." Hermione gave Cat a set of keys and explained where her gray Honda Accord was parked.

"I can't promise to return it in the same condition," she warned, touched by her generosity.

"Your safety matters most," Hermione declared. "Please, take it."

"Thank you."

"Security's here." Gray unsheathed his weapon. "Catriona, I'll cover you. You focus on getting to the car. Got it?"

"You'd better keep up, Michaelson, because I'm not leaving without you."

He arched a brow. "Yes, ma'am."

As soon as Hermione had locked herself in the bathroom, they exited the condo and inched to where the tall hedge ended. Gray was in the lead. "The guard is approaching the van in his security vehicle. Get ready."

Sweat trickled beneath her collar and between her shoulder blades. *God, it's me—* She didn't need to introduce herself anymore. He already knew her name. *I'm trusting You to lead us and guide us, to not forsake us.* Olivia had shared that particular Scripture during her own ordeal, and it had stuck with Cat.

Gray gave the unspoken signal, and they sprinted across the blacktop. She heard the ensuing commotion, the shouts and gunning of an engine. Cat kept her gaze on the Honda door. She'd lose precious seconds getting it unlocked. The unmistakable sound of a gunshot blasted her ears, and she ducked.

"Don't stop!" Gray commanded.

He crouched near the trunk and returned fire. The bullet pinged off the bumper.

Cat jammed the key into the lock. "Let's go," she urged.

Diving inside, she reached across and tugged the lock on his side. Gray dropped onto the seat, slammed the door and rolled down the window.

She gunned the Honda into Reverse. The van roared off the curb and rocketed toward them, leaving the security guard in its wake.

Cat jammed the gearshift into Drive and pressed hard on the gas pedal. The older car responded, and they sped through the complex. She executed a sharp right turn onto the city's thoroughfare. Rush hour had passed, so traffic was light. They were headed into the historic district. Tighter roads, lower speed limits and pedestrians awaited.

"Pike. It's Michaelson. Perps are in pursuit." He detailed their location.

Cat couldn't make out the detective's side of the conversation. The van's headlights flicked on and temporarily blinded her. One by one, the light poles came on as the sky transitioned from baby blue to periwinkle.

"Understood."

Sliding the phone back into his pocket, he maintained his grip on the gun and his gaze on the side mirror.

"Winthrop finally reached Jacksonville and is at the station demanding to see me."

"Convenient." She blasted through a yellow-verging-on-red light. The van surged forward, grinding against her bumper. Gripping the wheel, she pushed the speed almost double the posted limit. They left the commercial businesses behind. Houses built over a century ago crowded both sides of the street.

"The sedan they used to abduct Bianca was located. No info there. It was stolen. The bald guy with the intriguing scar? They input the sketch and got a hit—Axel Olufsen. He's a repeat offender based in Chicago. Pike's searching for any known connections to crime organizations. They're also on the lookout for credit card purchases linked to him."

A thought that had occurred to her at Hermione's pressed for attention. "If Tabitha is my mother, then Bianca's telling the truth. We're half sisters."

There was a beat of silence. "Go on."

"If I were to let them capture me, I would be taken to her. I could help her escape."

"That is a noble idea, Catriona." There was an undertone of anger in his voice she didn't understand. "There are too many unknowns. The risks would be astronomical."

"I don't want to put myself in harm's way, but my training as a marine and law enforcement officer will enable me to help her."

"The answer is no."

Disbelief bubbled up. "I don't recall asking you for permission."

The car shuddered with yet another assault from behind, and it veered toward the grassy median. Cat yanked the wheel to the right and nearly sideswiped a turning car. An angry honk trailed after them.

"We'll revisit this later," she gritted out, funneling all her concentration on not killing anyone, including themselves.

"You can be sure of it."

Catriona's idea disturbed him, deeply. He liked the courageous marine and couldn't bear the thought of her at the mercy of immoral creeps. It was bad enough that his protectee was in their grips.

Another bullet blasted toward them, grazing the metal side. "They're aiming for tires." One well-positioned shot would end this pursuit in a heartbeat.

"Suggestions?" She nodded to the thickening traffic and sea of red taillights ahead. Signs jammed into the ground advertised a summer concert series.

"How close are we to the waterfront?"

"A couple of blocks."

"I say we ditch the car and use this crowd to our advantage."

She considered his plan. "I'm on board with that. Hang on."

Jerking the wheel, she shot through a break in the median, crossed two lanes and entered a side street.

"Perfect timing," he said, twisting in his seat. "They got delayed by a semitrailer truck."

They whizzed past the parade of grand homes, navigating the residential area at excess speeds and making multiple changes in direction. The van was nowhere in sight.

"I'm glad you're the one driving," he said, shifting his weight into the turns.

His praise earned a grin. "I excelled at police driving school."

"It shows."

"There." Slamming on the brakes, she quickly parallel parked the car between a motorcycle and box truck. Across the way, vivid banners identified the building as a children's museum.

In moments, they were jogging along the uneven sidewalk. He could taste salt in the air. The distant thump of drums carried through the night. A vehicle slowly approached, high beams blinding them. He seized her hand and pulled her between a home's wide concrete stairs and an azalea bush.

"It's them," she murmured, unease threading through her voice. "They had to have seen the Honda."

"We'll wait a few minutes, then get lost in the concert crowd."

Five minutes passed, and they returned to the sidewalk with their hands still joined. Even with the danger nipping at their heels, he noticed her palm fit neatly into his, her fingers were long, like a piano player's, and her skin was soft and supple… Surprising, given the nature of her job.

"Let's take Front Street," she said, nodding to the approaching four-way juncture.

The lights from the quirky shops, bars and restaurants they passed glinted on Catriona's bright locks. Her red hair was a beacon in the darkness. He scanned the people on the sidewalks and spotted a couple lounging near a shop entrance.

"Excuse me, sir. I'll give you ten bucks for your hat."

The man and woman looked them over before exchanging a confused glance.

"Make it twenty." He fished a bill from his wallet and held it out. "My girlfriend forgot hers. She didn't take the time to fix her hair and is feeling self-conscious."

Catriona giggled and snuggled into his side. "Green's my favorite color," she said hopefully.

Gray sucked in a steadying breath, ignoring the desire to hold her close. "We haven't come across any clothing shops yet."

With a shrug, the stranger agreed. Playing his part of attentive boyfriend, Gray turned to her and carefully situated the hat atop her hair, making sure none of it was visible. Her head was tipped up, her eyes locked on his face, and he couldn't resist cupping her cheek. He slowly swept his thumb across her freckles. The growing need to be near her, to take their relationship further, spelled trouble.

Trouble. Another woman's face flashed before his eyes. Her face was twisted in anger.

"She hated my job," he murmured, lowering his hand and staring unseeing at the street.

"Gray?" Catriona's voice seemed to come through a tunnel.

More memories bombarded him, opening up old wounds. "Angel, my ex-fiancée. She had her heart set on being an army ranger's wife." They'd met at a charity marathon in the early years of his career. "We dated for four years. Between my field training and her pursuit of a law degree, we didn't spend as much time together as I would've liked. I thought marriage was the answer to our problems." In hindsight, he realized their misery would've followed them into married life.

"She broke off the engagement after your accident?"

Catriona's question dispersed the fog clouding his brain. Gray was unable to read her expression. She was good at cloaking her feelings, but he'd made a profession of interpreting others' true thoughts and motives.

"She bided her time, waiting to see if the army was going to keep me or not."

There…a spark of anger in her eyes. "I hope she waited until you'd fully recuperated."

He nodded. "Five weeks into my gig with the Winthrops."

"It's not a recent heartbreak, then," she said, her gaze probing.

"My heart is intact," he said with confidence. Somewhere in the recesses of his mind, there came a warning that it might not remain so for long.

The live music paused, followed by applause and cheers. "Let's go."

No time to dawdle. If their pursuers had seen the abandoned Honda, they would come in search of them.

The closer they got to the concert area, the denser the crowd became. The streets were closed to vehicle traffic. At the juncture of Front and

Market, vendors sold everything from glow sticks to smoothies. Both he and Catriona studied the passing faces, on alert for the three they'd seen before and others who looked suspicious.

The stage had been set up in a square bordered on both sides with businesses. The Cape Fear River formed a natural dead end. A massive ship's lights were visible on the opposite side, and Catriona informed him it was the USS *North Carolina*. She had to get close to his ear in order to be heard above the music.

The stage lights lit up much of the area, but there were dark swaths where their pursuers could conceal themselves. Shadowed passageways between buildings created more problems. He was second-guessing this decision.

He leaned close. "Let's keep moving." They'd find a temporary place to hunker down and await local authorities. Pike was supposed to have alerted Wilmington PD. So far, he hadn't seen a single law enforcement officer.

She stiffened, angling her head so the cap brim masked her profile. "Axel's here. Two o'clock."

The bald man was staring straight at them. No, at Catriona. The hunger in his eyes set Gray's blood on fire. Axel wasn't going to get her. He'd have to kill Gray first.

"Might as well lose the hat," he muttered. "He's seen it now."

She dropped it in a waste bin.

He interlaced his fingers with Catriona's and headed deeper into the crowd. The pavement beneath his feet thrummed with the beat. The attendees sang along with the lead singer. Some swayed, arms aloft. Others twisted to the rhythm. Their progress was painstaking, as not many willingly shifted to let them pass. Catriona held tightly to his hand. At times, she clutched his shirt to keep from getting separated.

Finally, when they were even with the stage, he saw an opening.

They left the square and hurried along a walkway bordered by the courthouse on their right and the river on their left. "You familiar with this area?" he said, glancing over his shoulder. No sign of Axel.

"Familiar enough," she said, her gaze darting back and forth. "There's a small park ahead and a hotel beyond that."

"We're exposed here."

A gunshot rang out, and Gray felt a puff of air inches from his cheek. Before he could shield Catriona, she pushed him toward the water's edge.

FOURTEEN

Cat couldn't return fire. There were innocent people nearby. Gray vaulted over the dock railing and, balancing on the edge, helped her over. The expanse between the dock and the triple-decker tour boat was difficult to judge. Axel fired on them again, bullets pinging against the metal and missing them by inches. They wanted to take out Gray, of course. A minor injury would slow her down and make it easier for them to catch her.

They leaped at the same time. Cat missed the target by a belt's width. Her body slammed into the hull and started sliding downward. Her fingers scrabbled against the slick siding. Gray seized her wrist with both hands and hauled her unceremoniously onto the deck.

"Come on," he urged, helping her to her feet and leading her around the stern to the opposite side.

Heavy thumps and exclamations announced

Axel and another man's arrival. Gray pointed to the stairs. Cat preceded him to the second level.

"Locked," she said, rattling the handle. It was either break down the door and enter the unoccupied dining space or continue to the top level.

He pointed to the sky, so she continued upward. The vessel was in the outer periphery of the stage lights, and the play of light and shadow played tricks with her eyes. The music started up again. The blaring beat and crowd's collective voices gave their pursuers an advantage.

She followed Gray down the length of the boat, using the skinny space between the bench seats and the see-through railing.

Were the goons bringing up the rear? Or had they navigated to the opposite set of stairs?

There was no time to confer with Gray about the best plan.

Sprinting to the engine room, where she assumed Gray meant to find cover, she didn't see the enemy coming. A man jumped from the engine room roof—the shaggy-haired one who'd manhandled her in the cottage. His momentum and weight took Gray to the floor. He stomped on his wrist, forcing Gray's hold on his gun to go slack.

Cat reached for her own weapon, tucked into her rear waistband. Her fingertips had barely brushed the grip when someone slammed into her from behind and shoved her flush against the engine room door. Her forehead bounced off the weathered wood, and she cried out as zip ties were slipped over her wrists and yanked tight enough to tear her skin. Alarm stole the air from her lungs.

Calm down. They haven't won yet.

She couldn't hear what was happening to Gray above the concert festivities. He wouldn't give up without a fight, and neither would she.

Cat slammed her head against her captor, her skull connecting with his. An ugly oath ripped from his lips. She used the momentary surprise to push back with her body, knocking him away and spinning to face him.

His bald head gleamed. Axel.

Having her hands secured behind her messed with her balance. Instead of running, she bulldozed him. He didn't go down. He smacked against the plexiglass half wall, the thick ledge even with his midback. She landed against him, and his growl of fury blasted her with heat.

Cat backpedaled and tripped, sitting down hard. He lunged for her.

Clenching her shoulders in a bruising grip, he towed her upright. Sweat beaded on his skin. His mouth was an angry slash.

"If it were up to me," he growled, "I'd sink you right now. You're more trouble than you're worth."

He shoved her toward the same stairs she and

Gray had used. She deliberately stumbled and fell to her knees. Twisting around, she craned her neck for a glimpse of him. Was he okay?

The two men were still engaged in battle, landing punches—

Pain exploded in her face as Axel's boot slammed into her. She keeled onto her side, the splintered floor scraping her cheek and the two figures in the corner tilting wildly. She couldn't move. The shock was too great. Her stomach revolted as the wretch grabbed a fistful of her hair and wrenched her upright.

A gasp was ripped from her as the barrel of his gun dug into her ribs, and he brought his face to hers. "You will stop fighting me, you hear?"

Cat swallowed several times, trying to keep the sickness at bay. "Y-yes."

He tugged her hair again, and moisture sprang to her eyes. "You'd better mean it."

Axel forced her farther down the center aisle and farther away from Gray. Her sluggish mind struggled to find a solution.

His opponent wasn't a basic, hired lackey. He'd matched Gray blow by blow, moves mirroring and deflecting his own. Out of the corner of his eye, he saw Axel's boot connect with Catriona's face. He saw her neck crack to the side. Saw her topple to the ground and stay there.

Something inside him snapped. *Enough.*

He thrust forward and used his flattened hand to strike his attacker's throat at the precise spot and angle. The goon's eyes rolled back, and he folded to the ground.

Gray frisked him for weapons and tossed a knife and gun overboard. Snatching his own from the ground, he ran after the fleeing thug and Catriona.

He reached the top of the stairs and spotted them on the middle deck landing. The way Axel held her suggested he had a gun to her side.

"Stop!" Gray commanded.

As he spied the weapon trained on him, Axel's face hardened. "Try it, and she's dead."

"You do that, and your asking price plummets."

He descended a step, risking a glance at Catriona. Her arms were bound behind her. Her hair was disheveled and her lip busted.

"I'm not the greedy one," Axel shot back.

"Let her go," Gray casually suggested, taking another step down. "Convince your puppet master to name his price. Winthrop's willing and eager to pay for his daughter's safety. Aren't you ready to leave this cat-and-mouse game behind?"

He paused, and Gray believed he was actually considering it.

Then he whipped the gun in his direction and pulled the trigger. Gray barely registered the hit as Axel swooped his arm beneath Catriona's knees and propelled her backward over the railing.

Gray's entire body flinched.

Her scream trailed behind her, punctuated by a splash.

Was he trying to *drown* her?

Axel jumped in after her.

Gray skidded down the stairs and launched himself off the boat. He hit the water seconds after the others. For a moment, the black depths disoriented him.

He had to get to Catriona. *Lord Jesus, please lead me to her.*

Breaking the surface, he dragged in air, shoved the hair out of his eyes and twisted in a complete circle. The large boat blocked the concert lights, thickening the shadows. He heard splashing near the boat's bow and sliced through the opaque water.

Axel had dragged Catriona to a long ramp and was shoving her onto it.

"Catriona!" he called, pushing himself to go faster.

Axel waved his gun in her face and shouted something unintelligible.

He wasn't going to reach her in time.

I can't fail her like I failed Bianca.

His side throbbed with each long stroke, but he forged ahead.

Catriona gave one last-ditch effort to free herself, flopping over onto her back and locking her ankles around Axel's neck before he could exit the river.

He hammered her shins with the gun grip. She refused to release him, buying Gray precious time.

At the same moment Gray looped his arm around Axel's neck, Catriona relaxed her hold. Gray submerged the man and told her to run.

"I'm not leaving you!"

Axel struggled to get free. Gray wasn't going to drown the man, only weaken him enough to be taken into custody. Pounding footsteps heralded the arrival of Axel's partner, who'd woken from the sleep Gray had put him in.

"Leave him," she urged.

Gray shoved him away and crawled onto the ramp. With a steadying hand on Catriona's arm, he ran with her to the dock gate and kicked it open. A glance over his shoulder showed the shaggy-haired man assisting Axel.

Water sluiced from their clothes onto the pavement. They dodged a jogger with his dog.

"He shot at you," she said, panting. "How did he miss?"

Gray wasn't going to correct her assumption until they'd reached safety. "We have to find a taxi and get to the police station."

"Through here." She changed direction and headed across a parking lot to a sprawling, multilevel redbrick shopping complex. "We'll take the stairs up to Front Street."

They took the open-air staircase to the next level, which emptied into a winding brick hallway with shops tucked in odd corners. They almost collided with an elderly woman, who took one look at them and retreated into the jewelry store.

"This way." Catriona nodded to another door.

He opened it for her. "We've got to get those zip ties off."

They darted across a courtyard, startling restaurant patrons enjoying a late supper. Through another door they sailed, taking yet another set of stairs to the street level. They entered a cobblestone area. The shops had false fronts to look as if they were outside.

"There's the exit."

Gray slowed his pace. "Just a second." Cocking his head to the side, he indicated the greeting card and paper shop. "Follow me."

The aisles were fortunately empty. The clerk looked up from her book and promptly dropped it on the counter.

Gray held up his hand. "Sorry for frightening you, but my friend and I have run into some trouble." He indicated the zip ties. "Do you have a pair of scissors?"

Her eyes unblinking, the clerk pointed a shaky finger to a container holding pens and other writing instruments. Gray snagged the scissors and cut the ties.

"Thank you, Lacey," he said, reading her badge. "You should go into your office, lock the door and call the police."

"Gray!" Catriona snagged his fingers with crushing intensity. "You're bleeding."

He saw the red seeping through his sodden shirt. "We'll tend it later."

She frowned, clearly torn. The overhead lighting illuminated her grazed, swollen cheek and bruised lip. He burned with indignation. Making Axel pay was not a priority, he reminded himself. Besides, Catriona was the epitome of resilience.

He told the people they encountered to return to the shops, find the clerk or manager and hunker down in the offices until authorities arrived.

"Gray, look."

Striding through the Front Street entrance was the skinny man who'd chased her in the park. He made no effort to conceal the Beretta in his possession.

They changed direction, thinking they could return to the intermediate level and leave by way of a side street. But Shaggy Hair shoved through that door. Where was Axel?

The only choice was to go up more stairs to the balcony level. They entered the first shop they encountered—gemstones and geodes sparkled amid clear glass cases.

"Can I help—" The short gentleman had emerged from behind the counter, only to stop short. "I don't want any trouble."

"Is there another exit?" Catriona asked, pulling her weapon and checking if the ammo was dry enough to use.

He backed up. "N-no. Just the one set of stairs."

Grimacing, she returned the weapon to her waistband. "I think it's too far gone."

"While mine's at the bottom of the river." He'd managed to hold on to it until his scuffle with Axel.

Seeing the clerk's escalating fear, Catriona flashed her military ID and quickly explained the situation. She hustled him into his office and told him to barricade himself inside and call the police. Catriona crouched behind the counter. Gray hid behind the largest display with an opaque stand.

They heard the thud of boots ascending the stairs. Judging by the ensuing activity, the men had split up to sweep the various shops.

Their guy entered with caution and approached Gray's hiding spot. Catriona's gaze locked onto Gray, and he could read the warning written on her features.

The thug stopped. Catriona slowly reached for a paperweight perched on the counter near her head. He shook his head and glared at her. She arched a defiant brow and made hand motions she hoped he understood.

Popping to her feet, she lobbed the paper-weight. There was an ensuing thwack and grunt.

Gray left the display and tackled the man. They fought for control of the weapon, and he had the upper hand until his opponent punched him in the wounded side.

A searing sensation radiated outward, and he lost his grip. His weapon slipped out of his grasp, and his enemy gained control of it. The momentary distraction cost him. Suddenly, he was staring death in the face.

FIFTEEN

Catriona's heart nearly stopped. Time slowed. The enemy hunched over Gray and pointed his gun at his chest. His finger hovered over the trigger.

In that moment, she knew she could not watch this man die. Could not lose him.

Snagging a heavy flower vase from the counter, she swung it in a wide arc and connected with the side of his head.

He faltered. Gray shifted upward and struck the man's chin with his palm. The blow sent him reeling. They grabbed the weapon and ran, luring him and his partner to the exit stairs and away from the shoppers.

Sirens greeted them when they stumbled onto a side street. They ran toward the sound.

Cat looked back and saw the men exit the shopping complex and scan the street. The old white van rolled up, Axel at the wheel, and they got in.

Gray's arm circled her waist, and he urged her around the corner and out of sight. Red and blue lights flickered over the pedestrian-filled street. Three police cruisers were parked in front of the entrance, and an officer conversing with onlookers noticed their approach. Catriona surrendered the weapon they'd taken from their attacker and quickly explained the situation. She flashed her ID. Learning that she was a military police officer lent her credence in his eyes.

She noticed Gray had gone quiet and was practically weaving on his feet.

"Please, can you take us to the nearest hospital? He's been shot."

The officer ushered them into his back seat and radioed command while maneuvering through the crowd. He put out a BOLO on the white van.

"I saw faded letters on the side," she told him, buckling in. "*ATE* was all I got."

He nodded. "Hang in there, Mr. Michaelson. The hospital's less than a ten-minute ride from here."

Gray lifted his head from the seat. "I appreciate the ride." He met her gaze. "It's fine."

Cat wasn't convinced. The blood had spread, and they hadn't yet had a chance to inspect the wound. Being exposed to the river water wasn't going to help.

He threaded his fingers through hers. "You're going to need medical attention, as well."

She nearly brought his hand to her cheek and

nuzzled it. Startled, she extricated herself. "I wasn't shot at close range."

Those moments on the boat would go down as some of the most terrifying of her life. She hadn't anticipated Axel's desperation. It made her very scared for Bianca.

At the hospital, Cat was released within the hour. Gray's injury was worse than he'd let on, but deemed superficial. It had carved out a hunk of flesh at his waist that would leave a gnarly scar if he didn't seek a plastic surgeon's treatment. He was started on a regimen of antibiotics and given extensive instructions on wound care.

She felt a rush of relief when he emerged wearing a clean set of blue scrubs. Relief and something deeper, something unsettling. How he had become important to her in such a short time was beyond comprehension.

I don't want to care about him, Lord. I don't know how to let someone in. Besides, he's only here temporarily. Once he locates Bianca, he'll return to Chicago. He probably sees me a younger sister, anyway.

"Where did you score those?"

"The nurses gave them to me."

"Why am I not surprised?" she muttered.

"I thought they'd give you some." His brows tugged together. "I'll go ask—"

"Don't bother." She'd rather wear her damp, stinky clothes than take a pity handout. "Pike arrived and briefed the local LEOs. She's our ride back to Jacksonville."

Police would return Hermione's Honda, and Cat's car would undergo a thorough inspection before it was returned.

They both got into the back seat without conscious thought, and Pike muttered something beneath her breath that made Cat feel like a teenager with her beau. No one seemed inclined to chat. The radio was tuned to a jazz station, and the mellow music lulled her into a relaxed state. Businesses and houses flashed by, and her body nestled more firmly into the cushions. Sometime later, voices and bright light shining full in her face roused her.

Her eyes blinked open, and the human heater beneath her cheek shifted. She was curled into Gray's side, her head against his chest and her arm slung over his stomach. How? When? Why did she want to stay in this spot indefinitely?

He trailed his fingers over her hair. "Catriona? We've reached the hotel."

Cheeks scorching, she sat upright and averted her face. "I don't remember hearing anything about a hotel."

They were parked beneath an expansive overhang. Cement planters flanked a rotating door, and a valet podium was emblazoned with a popular chain emblem.

"It's a temporary solution. Axel and his crew

had to have followed us to the rental house and planted the tracker."

"Why didn't they attack that night?"

"High visibility," he surmised. "On a central, busy road close to the sheriff's department. Tough to ambush. That's why I chose it."

"Yet they undoubtedly managed to get a tracker in my car," she said.

Through the multiple floor-to-ceiling windows, she glimpsed Pike at the desk. Cat's head felt swimmy, and she would give a lot of money for a long, hot shower, clean clothes and a steak. She wouldn't complain if a baked potato swimming in butter and sour cream accompanied it.

"Easier to manage that than to carry out a limp body."

His voice broadcast sheer exhaustion. Cat finally risked a glance at him. His hair hung in his eyes, and the beginning of a beard darkened his chiseled jaw. There was nothing in his expression that hinted at the intimacy of the car ride. Had he hated having her close? Had he endured it because he hadn't wanted to disturb her?

"You need rest."

His lips curved. "I need food."

She sighed. "Same."

Pike returned to the car, opened the driver's door and leaned in. "I got you adjoining rooms. We'll enter through the side."

"What about our belongings?"

"Someone from the department will go to the rental house tomorrow."

A silver late-model Jaguar slid to a stop beside the podium, and the uniformed driver opened the rear door. A second vehicle, a hulking black Hummer, parked behind it. Two men packing heat stood guard.

Pike turned to watch as a man emerged. He buttoned his suit jacket and glanced around.

"Winthrop," Cat breathed.

He carried himself with the assurance that his will would be obeyed.

Beside her, Gray tensed. "What's he doing here?"

Pike wasn't around to answer. She'd left them to confront him. Their conversation filtered through the open driver's door.

"You were told to stay away," Pike declared.

"I was discreet." Winthrop looked down his nose at her. "No one followed me."

"You can't guarantee that."

Cat opened her door and got out. Wayne Winthrop owed her answers.

Winthrop's gaze shifted past the diminutive detective and landed on Cat. His eyes widened. His nostrils flared. His Adam's apple bobbed.

The nonverbal cues were telling. He'd lied about Bianca not having a sibling.

Gray paced between the kitchen and living area. They had gotten an actual one-bedroom suite for Catriona, with an adjoining double room for Gray. He listened as the business-man—his boss, he'd do well to remember—explained why he'd denied the existence of an-other child. He hadn't wanted to dredge up dam-aging news that might tarnish his late wife's memory.

And affect continued sales of her records? he wondered. What was Winthrop truly worried about? The public's perception of the jazz queen or their willingness to continue opening their wallets?

Gray instinctively knew this wasn't a stand-up guy. Which begged the question—why did he work for him?

"She wanted to keep me," Catriona stated. "Hermione was adamant on that point."

She was seated in the corner armchair, her hands folded tightly in her lap. The serene pose was offset by the challenge in her gaze and the defiant angle of her chin. Her freckles were in stark contrast to her pale skin. Gray could imag-ine her state of mind, the physical toll of their ordeal now compounded by this emotional roller coaster. He wished he had the right to go to her and offer comfort. Those precious moments in the car, when she'd unconsciously sought his warmth and closeness, would stick with him.

Winthrop was a master at masking his true feelings. More skilled than Catriona, even. But there were cracks. Visible cracks brought on by jet lag, the lack of control and the ongoing danger to Bianca.

"That's a private matter, young lady."

She removed the photograph of Tabitha from her back pocket and slapped it on the coffee table. Hot color suffused her cheeks. "For years, I have searched for clues that would lead me to my family. I've hit one roadblock after another. Someone went to great lengths to conceal my birth parents' identities."

He refused to look at the photograph. Tugging at his tie to loosen it, he said, "I feel for your plight—"

"Your initial reaction to seeing me mirrored Hermione's."

Abruptly leaving the couch, he sliced the air with his hand. "You think you're Tabitha's long-lost daughter simply because you have red hair and green eyes? The media will spin your claims, and not in your best interest. You'll be portrayed as a pathetic woman desperate to attach her identity to the world's most beloved jazz singer."

The color drained from her face. "I hadn't planned on making my quest for answers public. I'm not after money."

"That's good, because you aren't getting any."

Gray balled his fists. "Her eyes aren't an ordinary green, Winthrop. Take a closer look. Look familiar?"

The other man's eyes narrowed. "I don't appreciate your tone, Michaelson. Keep in mind you're on thin ice. Under your watch, I lost my daughter, and one of my finest employees wound up dead. I'm within my right to terminate your employment."

Catriona stood to her feet. "Gray has risked his life trying to protect me. I wouldn't want anyone else by my side. He's the best."

"Thank you," Gray said softly, touched by her impassioned defense. "Look, my employment status isn't the point. Bianca was obviously convinced Catriona was the half sister she'd been searching for. Have your people look into her actions prior to this trip. How did she learn of this secret baby? She had to have had help with the investigation. Did she turn to a trusted friend or hire a professional?"

"None of those answers will lead us to her," Winthrop ground out, thrusting both hands through his hair. Pike arrived then and placed twin white sacks on the kitchen counter. In her wake, mouthwatering scents filled the room. Hamilton, one of Winthrop's personal bodyguards, remained in the hallway standing watch. Gray had apparently hired the guy last year, yet he remembered nothing about him. He would make a point of having a chat with him later. The more information he pulled in from varied sources, the clearer the picture of his life would become.

"I feel like I haven't eaten in weeks. What did you bring us?" Catriona said.

"What you asked for—steaks, baked potatoes and yeast rolls as big as your fist."

"I didn't think you'd actually spring for it."

"After everything you two have been through, I figure you deserve it." She started unloading the boxes. "I have enough for you, Mr. Winthrop."

"No, thank you." He shot a lingering glance at Catriona before heading out. "I'll be in touch."

Gray got the feeling his boss was up to something, something that wouldn't benefit anyone other than himself.

Pike joined them for the meal. Gray took his plate to the sofa, while the women shared the minuscule table. The television relayed the local news, and everyone pretended to be engrossed in it. At least, he pretended. His mind was busy processing the details of their latest confrontation. There had been some close calls. He would've liked to banish the replay of Axel's treatment of Catriona.

When Pike left an hour later, Catriona announced she'd like to shower and go to bed. In other words, he needed to make himself scarce. Gray turned at the adjoining door and settled his hands on her shoulders. She looked up, her lips parting in surprise.

"How are you holding up?"

Her eyes clouded.

"This is dragging out too long. The authorities aren't even close to figuring out who's holding her hostage."

"They're looking into Axel's connections. They'll find something."

"What happens to her in the meantime?"

"Greed is driving them. Once they figure out they can't get to you, they'll call again with their demands."

"I pray you're right."

SIXTEEN

After washing away the grime, Cat changed into sweats and a T-shirt that Pike had picked up from a nearby discount store. Her body was sore and covered with bruises, but she no longer smelled like stale river water and sweat. Propped up on a ridiculous number of pillows, she stared at her phone screen. This internet image of Bianca was her favorite. It was a casual shot of the twenty-year-old…no makeup, hair lying in natural waves around her shoulders, a genuine smile brightening her features. She was beaming at her mother. *Their* mother?

Wayne had answered some of their questions about Bianca. She'd been a precocious child, often entertaining her family members with poetry recitations and songs. Bianca hadn't inherited Tabitha's talent, though, and they'd all suffered through her attempts to mimic her mother. She loved animals, and over the years had convinced them into letting her have a wide array, including gerbils, macaws and parrots, lizards, cats and even a banana king snake. She hated math and history. Science fascinated her, and she could occasionally be found flipping through interior design magazines.

The things he'd told them only whetted Cat's desire to know more. The rational, cautious part of her warned not to jump the gun. There was no concrete proof yet. But the lonely little foster kid she'd once been was jumping up and down, begging for it to be true.

A text came in from Olivia. She was worried about her. Why had she missed church yesterday and why hadn't she answered her calls? Cat debated what to tell her. In the end, she decided her friend deserved the truth. Olivia was no wilting violet. Marriage and pregnancy hadn't changed that.

Snuggling deeper into the pillows, she made the call. As expected, Olivia expressed dismay over her circumstances. Cat gently deflected her offer of help and asked for prayer instead.

Before dawn the next morning, Pike arrived with Cat's uniform, coffee and a box of assorted pastries.

Lifting the lid and letting Cat have first choice, she stared at her over the top of her glasses. "Are you sure you're up to working today?"

Not wanting to go into details, Cat took a bite of chocolate croissant and nodded. Gray knocked on the adjoining door, and she let him in. He took one look at her cammies and gave a resigned sigh. He understood her reasons, but he didn't like her decision.

"Have you informed your command what's going on?" Pike said, offering the box to Gray.

"Not yet," Cat replied.

"They aren't going to reprimand you for circumstances beyond your control."

Cat nearly choked on her coffee. If she only knew…

"How are you going to explain that?" Pike gestured to Cat's swollen, tender cheek.

"I'm going to tell them it's none of their business." Not in those exact words, of course.

"Are you driving us to the base?" Gray asked.

"Actually, Catriona's car has been cleared and delivered here." She fished a set of keys out of her pocket and placed them on the counter. "I will follow you to the base entrance, however. I'll have an escort waiting once your shift is over."

"You found a tracking device?"

"It's newer technology. My guys almost missed it. The perps snuck it beneath the carpet in your trunk." She dusted the crumbs from her hands into the sink. "My advice is to inform your command and ask for a week off. Hunker down here. It's not exactly a hardship. Have you seen the indoor pool?"

"I'm taking it day by day."

Pike shrugged. "I'll see you downstairs."

The door closed behind her, and Cat turned to Gray. "You don't have to accompany me, you know. You could watch television. Forget the pool. Not with your injury."

"I'm no good at sitting around twiddling my thumbs. Besides, I could use a new wardrobe." Waving his hand down the length of his blue scrubs, he flashed a smile that made her heart race.

"You look like one of those dashing TV doctors. My foster mom Dana was obsessed with a popular British one. Kurt teased her about it, going around faking an accent."

"You think I'm dashing?" He caught her hand, brought it to his lips and pressed a kiss to her knuckles. "Why, thank you, Sergeant."

His attempt at a British accent was even worse than her former foster dad's had been. "Take my advice. Don't try that again."

Could he see her pulse leaping at the base of her throat?

The twinkle in his eyes heated to a bonfire, and his thumb passed in a repetitive pattern over her fingers. Her gaze freely roamed his face, which mirrored the tug-of-war attraction she felt inside. Cat was stunned. He released her, only to settle his hand against her hip and draw her closer.

He lowered his mouth to hers in a featherlight

kiss. When he eased back, his eyes were dark and searching.

"Was that okay?"

Cat's throat was thick. She cupped his nape and pulled his face down to hers again, answering without words. The lingering, sweet-as-molasses kiss made her toes curl in her combat boots.

She left his embrace and backed away.

He let his hands fall to his sides. "Are we gonna talk about this?"

"What would be the point?"

He looked sad. "The timing…"

"The circumstances…"

Cat hadn't been looking to fall for someone. She would be a fool to risk her battered, lonely heart on a man with amnesia whose life and career were in another state.

"We're agreed, then," she said, snagging her uniform cover from the bar stool and rolling it between her hands. "No more of that."

He opened his mouth to speak, but her phone buzzed. "Pike's getting antsy."

Gray was quiet, almost brooding, on the way to the air station. She wasn't happy, either. Why had God brought him into her life?

At the military police office, he took her place behind the wheel and rolled down the window. "I'll be at the exchange or bowling alley if you need me."

"Bowling? With your injury? Did the nurses okay that?"

"The movie theater, then. I'll save you some popcorn."

She watched him drive away, wishing she could watch a movie with him and share a box of red licorice. Maybe he'd hold her hand.

Cat banished the thoughts and reported for duty. Paired up with Miller again, they responded to a domestic dispute and were forced to take the military member into custody. Her mood plummeted. Why would someone with a family to love and care for throw it all away over petty disagreements? The military lifestyle did present its unique set of challenges, but lots of couples made it work. Take Brady and Olivia, for example. Or Julian and Audrey. Or Cade and Tori, whom she didn't see often since they were stationed in California. If Cat were to ever find a loving, supportive partner, she wouldn't take him for granted.

That kiss whispered through her mind, wreaking havoc with her thoughts.

"We're being summoned to the armory," Miller told her, making a U-turn in the commissary parking lot.

Cat didn't think anything about it, until she saw Staff Sergeant Taube stationed outside, his jaw hard, eyes flinty and muscular arms folded tightly across his chest.

"What's eating him?"

"I don't know," she said, reluctantly exiting the vehicle.

"Sergeant Baker." He jerked his head to the right and marched down the sidewalk.

Miller gave her a commiserating glance. She belatedly noticed several marines crowded into the building's doorway, staring holes into her. Cat's insides erupted into chaos. Her skin became slicked with sweat, and it had nothing to do with the summer sun and North Carolina humidity. She was flung into the past, to another base, where the men and women she'd faithfully served alongside had regarded her as garbage. Sergeant Craft had painted her to be a desperate, lovesick woman willing to dishonor the uniform and the Corps with wild lies. He'd gone to great lengths to cover his crimes, to discredit her, and she'd felt powerless.

The croissant she'd eaten threatened to come up.

She lengthened her strides. "Sir, if I may ask—"

"Not here."

This was bad. So bad he couldn't discuss it within earshot of the others.

They came to a group of picnic tables shaded by several trees. He climbed onto the first one, perching on the table and propping his boots on the bench.

He patted the spot beside him. "Have a seat, Baker."

Although unusual, she complied. He proceeded to pull out his phone and hand it to her.

"There's something you need to see."

He started the video, which appeared to be a local newsclip. Wayne Winthrop stood outside the police department. He addressed the problems in his marriage and confirmed the rumors about Tabitha.

"This woman—Catriona Baker—is not my daughter."

Cat's fingers tightened on the phone. Winthrop held up a photo of her in uniform.

"At this date, no proof exists that she is my late wife's daughter." He stared directly into the camera. "I will not now, nor will I ever, pay a ransom in the event she's taken."

Her lungs emptied of breath, and her head felt too light for her body.

"To the men who have Bianca, call me. I'll double your asking price. Just please—" He faltered, and his bravado slipped. "Don't hurt her."

The shot cut to the newsroom, where the anchors began discussing the revelations and what they meant. They also discussed her, speculating what she could want from the Winthrop family.

She saw squiggly lines, and she flushed hot.

Taube took the phone from her, put his hand on her neck and gently urged her head down between her knees. "Breathe. In and out. Slow and steady. You're no weak debutante. Don't change my opinion of you now."

Cat focused on her breathing like he said, until her vision cleared. She slowly sat up.

"Time to fill me in, Baker."

She took in his expression, surprised and grateful there was no judgment, no blame. When she'd told him everything starting with the night Bianca was abducted, he whistled.

"That's why your face looks like you ate concrete?"

She lifted her hand to her cheek and shuddered, recalling Axel's assault.

"You didn't have to shoulder this alone."

"I didn't feel I had another choice."

His gaze seemed to see through her. "I heard bits and pieces of what happened in Okinawa."

Men loitered outside the armory, tossing curious glances their way.

"I was wary at first," Taube continued, "but I've watched how you conduct yourself. The Marine Corps is fortunate to have you."

Her eyes smarted. "Thank you."

"I don't buy that you're the love-crazy type. Why did you allow them to label you as such?"

"It's complicated."

He sighed. "This current situation is, too."

"I won't let it affect my performance."

"Your life is in danger, Baker. You can't pretend it's not." He unfolded himself from the table. "Take emergency leave. Keep yourself safe."

By the end of the day, everyone on New River and Camp Lejeune would know her name. Winthrop had seen to that.

"Emergency leave it is."

Catriona wasn't waiting impatiently on the curb as he'd expected. Nor was she chatting with other marines who milled about outside headquarters. Gray parked the car and went inside. The corporal behind the desk gave him a hooded stare.

"She left before lunch. Haven't seen her since."

"She's working on a case?"

"No, sir."

"Do you know where she might be?"

She hadn't responded to his texts, but he'd assumed she'd been busy.

"No, sir."

A young woman passing by overheard their exchange and waved him over. Pushing through the door, she pointed to the lone tree in the midst of a field. "She's over there."

"Thanks." Gray jogged along the sidewalk, then slowed when he reached the grass. She was seated cross-legged at the tree's base, and she had a book in her hands. Her regulation bun had been unraveled, and her hair rippled over her shoulders and hid her face. The camo backpack must hold her uniform and gear, because she'd changed into a filmy blouse, jeans and tennis shoes.

"Catriona."

She didn't immediately lift her face. Sliding in a bookmark, she closed the book and held it to her chest.

"How was your day?" Her voice sounded rough, raw.

"Better than yours, I think." He closed the distance between them and crouched before her. Gingerly he tipped up her chin. Her skin was pink and splotchy, her eyes bloodshot.

Alarm shot through him. "What happened?"

"I was forced to take leave."

Turning her face away, she picked up her phone and pulled up a video.

He watched it with increasing disgust.

"The entire world knows my name," she said, her tone detached. "The tabloids are already making wild claims. Soon, they will unearth what happened in Okinawa."

A breeze teased the branches, and dappled sunlight danced over her hair, creating a play of red and gold. The blouse was a shade hovering between gray and green, enhancing her unique eyes. She was so beautiful it hurt. He'd been enamored of her strength and courage and had forgotten she wasn't superhuman. She'd done nothing to deserve what happened with her previous command, and she hadn't deserved Winthrop's callous treatment.

Gray buried his fury, to be vented later. Catriona needed him.

He held out his hand. "Come with me."

Her brows tugged together. "I'm not ready to return to the hotel."

"I know."

She placed her hand in his and allowed him to help her up. He grabbed the backpack and, still holding her hand, walked her to the car. When they pulled into the base movie theater, she shot him a confused glance.

"Haven't you already seen a movie today?"

"There's no limit to how many you can see," he said lightly. "Besides, I only had one tiny popcorn. The clerk gave me a kid-size one. I'm sure of it."

He bought tickets to the comedy, and then proceeded to purchase the jumbo snack pack. Catriona's jaw dropped. "That's enough to feed a platoon."

The assortment of candies and chocolate, along with pretzels, popcorn and giant sodas, was the sort of indulgence a day like hers required. They found seats in the back. Because most of the air station's marines were getting off work and heading home for supper, they had the place mostly to themselves. The sugar and jokes perked her up, until they didn't, and the soft laughter turned to silent tears.

Gray put his arm around her and pulled close, stroking her hair while she wept.

He wished he could wipe away her grief, wished he could shield her from further hurt.

In the car afterward, she stared out the windshield. "How could he do this?"

"Wayne Winthrop lives to serve himself."

"Tabitha didn't stand up to him," she mused. "She didn't fight for herself. I suppose we have more in common than just our looks. Wayne's a bully, and so is Sergeant Craft."

He covered her hand. "Someday, when you decide the time is right, you'll take your claim to someone who will listen. I'll support you."

"From Chicago?"

He didn't remember much about his life there, and the prospect of leaving Catriona ripped a wound in his chest. But she hadn't indicated she wanted him to stick around. "You've heard of emails and video chats, I presume? Jacksonville has an airport."

She pursed her lips. "I could be stationed at Camp Pendleton by then. Or Twentynine Palms."

"Those places have airports."

"If you'd suggested a week ago that I'd willingly revisit the past, I would've laughed in your face."

"And now?"

"I have to ask myself a hard question. What's

more important? My career? Or seeing justice served?"

"'Trust in the Lord with all your heart, And lean not on your own understanding,'" he quoted. "'In all your ways acknowledge Him, And He shall direct your paths.' God will guide you."

"The Marine Corps is my life. My family. My home."

Gray wanted to reassure her that if she did pursue this, everything would turn out okay in the end. He wanted to tell her that she'd soon be reunited with her sibling. There were no guarantees.

"I felt the same about the Rangers." Ever since that significant memory of Angel resurfaced, bits and pieces of his past were becoming dislodged each day. He'd loved that life, what he remembered of it—the rigorous physical and mental demands, the brotherhood, the knowledge they lived each day to protect their country. He'd also thought he'd marry Angel and have a couple of kids. He couldn't help feeling he'd dodged a bullet on that last one. "It wasn't easy to start over. To dare dream of a different reality. You have to trust God's sovereign plan. He has plans for our good."

"*Trust* is a dirty word in my book."

He squeezed her hand. "You're going to get through this, Catriona. God will be leading you and protecting you. He'll be right by your side, and so will I."

SEVENTEEN

Catriona climbed the pool ladder and, wringing the excess water from her hair, retrieved her black halter dress from the table in the corner. The boisterous family she'd shared the indoor pool with had left ten minutes ago, and the ensuing silence was unsettling.

After pulling the cover over her swimsuit, she entered the small courtyard where Gray had retreated to take a call from his parents. He paced beside the wrought iron fencing. Bushes taller than him provided a natural boundary, blocking the full sunset that was turning the sky a stunning coral hue.

He ended the call as soon as he spotted her. "Feel better?"

Had she purged the nervous energy created by being confined to a hotel room for forty-eight hours? No. Was it fun swimming alone? Negative. Had it given her a break from the mind-numbing talk shows and reality television? Yes.

She tugged a heavy chair out and sat. "How did your parents take the news?"

"My mother is upset that we didn't interrupt their cruise. She's worried, obviously." He lowered his frame into the chair opposite. "That she didn't descend into hysterics is a good sign."

"And your dad?"

"The opposite of worried." His lips quirked. "I get the feeling he leaves that to my mother."

"Did you tell them you got shot?"

"Nah. I figured the crowbar-to-the-head thing was enough."

She nodded. "Along with not remembering them, the people who brought you into this world and raised you."

"Yeah."

Her thoughts strayed again to her own no-family situation. Pike had visited that morning, and they'd had a group video chat with Wayne to discuss a break-in at his home. His appearance testified to his spiraling loss of control. The expensive suit had looked as if it had been run beneath a car's tires, and his hair hadn't seen styling gel in days. There'd been no communication from the abductors.

Despite his callous actions, Cat had experienced a twinge of sympathy for him. She was growing increasingly concerned about Bianca, a young woman she'd never met but who might be the sister she'd longed for. Her subconscious was conjuring up movie-like nightmares each time she closed her eyes. It was the same scenario… Bianca was screaming for help, but Cat couldn't reach her.

"What are you thinking?"

"I'm wondering if Bianca is still alive."

His jaw tensed. "She's alive."

"They haven't called. What if they did something to accidentally cause her death?"

He shifted forward, his blue eyes intense. "Trust me, they aren't going to be careless with a high-value hostage. The break-in at the Winthrops' compound yesterday has to be connected."

"Wayne's stunt alerted every criminal in the greater Chicago area to the fact no one is home, and the majority of his security team is focused on his daughter's rescue."

"I don't think it's a random break-in." He shook his head. "Maybe we'll learn crucial information from Axel's acquaintances."

Pike had told them that morning that Axel was ex-military, and that Chicago PD planned on rounding up a handful of his buddies today.

He glanced at his watch. "I'm hungry. What are you in the mood for tonight? Pizza? A burger from the hotel restaurant?"

Was Bianca getting fed on a regular basis? Were her basic needs being met?

"You pick. I'm going to retrieve my things from the ladies' room."

Concern filling his eyes, he nodded. "I'll wait for you." Before she reached the pool-area door, his phone rang, and she heard him greet Fallon. He left the table to again pace beside the shrubs.

Cat pushed through the doors and walked swiftly through the humid room, keeping close to the lounge chairs as she bypassed the rectangular pool and entered the women's restroom. The room contained the usual amenities, plus showers and lockers. Cat dropped her used pool towels in the laundry container and located her locker. She opened the door and got out her backpack. When she turned to leave, she nearly jumped out of her skin.

A dark-haired woman wearing a staff uniform blocked her exit with a laundry cart piled high with sheets and towels. "I'm sorry for startling you, ma'am."

She pressed her hand to her chest. "It's okay. I'm jumpier than usual these days."

"Did you have a nice swim?"

"Yes, thank you."

Her ruby-red lips curved into a congenial smile. "You didn't happen to lose a phone, did you? I found one on this bench."

"I don't think so." Cat was typically careful with her device, but she'd had a lot on her mind lately. She checked the usual slot in her backpack.

Empty. She turned to look inside the locker again. "Maybe I forgot it in the room. What color is the case? Mine's black-and-white—"

The woman, whose name tag read Veronica, had rounded the cart, wielding a spray bottle. A fine mist was shot directly at Cat's face. It shot up her nose and in her mouth. She stumbled back. Opened her mouth to scream, only to receive another blast. Then another.

She sagged against the lockers. Her mind went fuzzy.

Veronica stuffed a rag in her mouth and shoved her to the floor.

Her muscles were heavy. Clumsy. Woozy and disoriented, Cat stayed on the ground. Her heart raced, slamming against her chest.

She'd been drugged.

Gray ceased his pacing and glanced at the pool visible through the glass doors. "Fallon, how long have we been talking?"

"Fifteen minutes, maybe. Why?"

Catriona had been gone longer than he'd thought. She hadn't mentioned taking a shower or anything else, only getting her things from the locker. He'd gotten caught up in the conversation.

"I have to go."

He ended the connection with no further explanation, a sense of foreboding spreading through his chest. Striding to the restroom door, he hesitated. He couldn't barge in without knowing there was an actual emergency. In the hallway, he waved down a passing guest.

"Excuse me, ma'am. My friend has been in the restroom for a while, and I'm getting worried. Would you mind checking on her?"

The young woman went inside and returned shortly. "Your friend must've left. There's no one in there."

Gray thanked her and called Cat's cell on his way to the elevators. Could she have seen him deep in conversation with Fallon and decided to go on up to the room? He got her voice mail just as he entered the elevator. He shoved his phone in his pocket and punched the floor number. Maybe she was in the shower, he rationalized.

But the suite was ominously empty. He checked the closet safe—her weapons were inside. Because his was at the bottom of the river, they'd returned to the rental cottage with an escort and retrieved her second weapon.

Tucking one of the guns in his waistband, he searched their floor's vending machine area. The hope that she was somewhere in this hotel and that they'd simply missed each other was fading fast. The front desk clerk denied seeing her. Frustration pounding at his temples, he turned a complete circle and surveyed the lobby.

Pike had reassured them she hadn't been followed on the trip from Wilmington, and he himself had watched for tails during their drive from the air station base on Tuesday evening. There were hundreds of hotels in Jacksonville and the surrounding coastal communities. No way could their enemy have the time or resources to check each one.

He needed to see her familiar face. If anything happened to her—

Gray had attempted to classify this as a typical guardian-protectee relationship, despite the fact Catriona was capable of defending herself. In fact, she'd saved him more often than he'd saved her. Still, he'd tried to maintain a certain professionalism. His growing attachment was proof he'd failed.

He'd kissed her. Grieved for and with her.

She had allowed him to see the sorrow she guarded so carefully and had turned to him for comfort. Those moments in the movie theater had shredded his heart and pieced it back together with a Catriona-shaped bandage.

Security professionals had warned him about this exact scenario. The bond growing between them couldn't be trusted. Could it?

Returning to the front desk, he demanded to know the location of the security office.

"Why don't I call someone for you—"

"A woman's life is in danger," he ground out, slapping the counter. "There's no time to waste."

The manager on duty emerged and listened to his brief explanation before escorting him to the security office. There, a single guard was watching animal videos on his phone instead of the security feeds. Gray barely held his temper in check as he quickly explained the danger.

While the manager summoned the authorities, the guard, whose name tag read Edwin, rewound the footage. Gray impatiently scanned the fuzzy images. There was no sign of her.

Gray tapped the upper right screen. "That woman pushing the laundry cart out of the pool room. She's struggling to manage it." As if it contained something heavier than linens. His throat closed up.

The guard replayed it. "I don't recognize that woman."

Gray's skin felt too tight for his bones. "Are you telling me she's new and you haven't met her yet, or she's an impostor?"

"I—I don't know," Edwin stammered.

The manager ended his call. "Police will be here shortly."

Edwin looked to the manager for help. "Is she legit?"

He paled. "I'm afraid she's not part of our hotel staff."

They'd gotten to her. This woman had posed as a hotel employee and somehow managed to sneak Catriona out of the building. How she'd done that, he was afraid to imagine. Gray pushed past the others and took off to where they'd last been seen. He should've waited and watched the entire footage, but seconds were precious.

It might already be too late.

EIGHTEEN

He burst through the outlying exit and into the employee parking lot, just as the woman in the footage hopped into an older-model red truck. The engine rumbled to life. Gray sprinted over and, grabbing for the door handle, saw that the passenger seat was empty. The driver's eyes widened. Then her red lips formed a grim line.

She slammed the gear into Reverse. Before she could press the gas, he saw the blankets in the truck bed. He saw a foot clad in a sandal peeking out from beneath them. Catriona.

His world tilted, and his vision blinked in and out.

Tires squealed against the pavement, and Gray had to leap out of the way to avoid his feet getting caught beneath them. The truck shot toward the adjacent side street.

Gray sprinted after it and grabbed hold of the truck's tailgate. His shoes dragged the ground. The sight of Catriona under those blankets kept his hands glued to the truck and gave his body the burst of strength it needed. He got his foot wedged into the bumper and sprang into the bed. His wounded side pulsed a dull, warning ache.

The truck swung onto the side street, and he braced his weight to avoid tumbling into Catriona. Through the rear windshield, he saw the driver glance over her shoulder. Her expression reflected utter resolve. What motivated her? Threats? Money? Loyalty?

When the truck straightened, he removed his weapon, crawled around Catriona and busted out the side window. They sped up. Swerved. He lost his grip and slammed into the bed's side wall. His lower back and side throbbed.

Up ahead, an intersection loomed. Would she slow down to merge with oncoming traffic?

Gray made his way again to the spot behind the side door, leaned around the frame and aimed his gun at the driver. "I'm not letting you take her," he growled. She slammed on the brakes.

He nearly went flying. The truck veered toward the curb.

Gray hunkered down and shielded Catriona seconds before they struck the curb, bounced onto the sidewalk and jostled over uneven terrain. As soon as the vehicle shuddered to a stop, he readied his weapon.

The woman bailed and sprinted toward the traffic. His first priority was Catriona's well-being, and he had no idea if others were waiting in the wings to assist in the abduction.

Ripping the covers from her, he checked her pulse and watched the rise and fall of her chest. She was pale and unresponsive, but she was alive.

He dropped the tailgate and, leaping to the ground, pulled her into his arms.

Police cruisers raced from the opposite direction, parking at odd angles to block the street.

"This woman needs medical attention," he shouted. "She's out cold, and I have no clue what's been done to her."

"Let's put her on the ground until paramedics arrive."

Gray didn't want to release her, but he complied, laying her gently on the grass and brushing the damp hair from her face. He held her hand between his and relayed the perp's description.

As the officers worked the scene around him, he kept his attention fixed on her.

Relief warred with worry. He prayed in fits and starts.

That was too close, Lord.

He could handle physical pain. He could deal with the confusion and frustration of having his memory wiped clean. He could recover from the loss of his security position, which was bound to happen. But the loss of Catriona would surely shatter him.

* * *

Cat burrowed deeper into the cushions. A firm brocade pillow supported her cheek, and a thin blanket covered her, staving off the arctic blast of air. She felt warm and floaty. Someone was stroking her hair, fingertips occasionally grazing her neck.

Her lids were heavy and her eyes gritty. She took in the coffee table, hotel informational folder and key cards, paper coffee cups and phone.

Memories rushed in, and she bolted upright.

"Catriona?" Gray placed the pillow on the coffee table and angled toward her. His blue eyes were large and dark. "Are you okay?"

Her hair slid forward into her eyes, and she pushed it behind her ears. "I don't feel so good."

She ran, slamming her knee against the low table on her sprint to the bathroom. Gray remained in the bedroom while she lost the contents of her stomach. Her reflection in the mirror told a tale of exhaustion and stress. She pressed cold, damp washcloths to her face.

When she emerged, he fetched her a frosty can of ginger ale.

"Thanks." She trudged back to the couch. "I'm as weak as a kitten."

He slid his hands in his pockets. "Do you remember what the doctor said?"

"Remind me."

He pulled out a dining chair and sat. "You should be back to your fighting form by tomorrow."

Sipping the soda, she looked at the clock and was astonished to see it was 1600 hours. She'd spent much of the night in the emergency room as they ran tests to determine the contents of that spray. They'd released her at ten that morning, and she'd promptly fallen asleep as soon as they'd reached the hotel.

Gray had watched her sleep. For hours.

"I—I'm sorry," she stammered. "I didn't know I was trapping you on the couch—"

His eyes warmed with emotion that both calmed and intrigued her. "I wasn't trapped. I left my spot a couple of times to eat and stretch my legs."

"Oh." So he'd wanted to be close.

She wanted him close. Why was he sitting across the room now that she was awake?

As if reading her thoughts, Gray left the chair, edged between the couch and coffee table and sat facing her. Their knees bumped together. He took her hand in his.

"How's your wound?" she said.

When she'd finally shaken the drug's effects, he'd recounted how he'd located her and prevented the abduction. That had been hours ago, yet she could still feel the sensation of the cold mist in her nose and the awful shutdown of her body.

"The same as when you asked last night and this morning."

"You reopened the wound." Had to have been painful.

"It's fine." He cradled her hand and caressed her skin with his thumb. "There are no signs of infection."

"I don't know why God is allowing this to happen," she said softly. "I'm leaning on Him more than ever before, so there's that. I used to begin my prayers like a business letter. I don't introduce myself anymore."

"He could be using this to orchestrate a family reunion."

"Maybe." She lifted her gaze to his. "I'm grateful you're with me."

Gray cupped her cheek. He leaned closer, and she parted her lips and closed her eyes in expectation. His kiss, when it finally came, whispered over her forehead. She heard him stand to his feet, felt the brush of his jeans against her knees.

When she opened her eyes, he was peering into the fridge and weighing his choices.

Cat pulled her feet to her chest and wrapped the blanket around her to ward off the chill. He wasn't rejecting her, she reminded herself. This wasn't another foster family who'd decided she wasn't a good fit.

He was being sensible, unlike her. *Get it together, Baker.*

Must be the aftereffects of the drug. According to the doctor, she'd been given an extremely high dose of a fast-acting sedative spray developed for children. Where "Veronica" had gotten her hands on it was a mystery.

Gray popped the tab of a caffeinated soda. "There's an officer stationed outside the door. He'll be there until we decide where we're going next."

"Where will that be?"

"Possibly a safe house."

"How did they find us?"

He perched on the edge of a stool. Keeping his distance. "Pike's convinced it was Winthrop. They must've tailed him here that first day and have been biding their time, patching together a plan."

"Did they catch the woman? Veronica?"

"No, but they have her vehicle. It's registered to someone named Vera Cross. Pike texted a half hour ago and asked if you felt like meeting her at the station. She found photographs inside Vera's residence that she'd like us to look at. I told her it would have to wait."

Cat stood to her feet so fast the room spun. "I'm ready now."

He set the can down with a thunk. "Catriona—"

"Every minute we're playing cat and mouse is another minute Bianca is at the mercy of these thugs. I'm going."

He looked resigned. "I'll get the keys."

* * *

Catriona had mentally retreated, leaving Gray to wonder if it was his fault. There was a tug-of-war inside him, and trying to temper his growing feelings with caution left him on edge.

"Take a look at this." Pike beckoned them over to her desk.

Catriona lifted the picture frame. "That's her, all right." Eyes narrowing, she studied the photo more closely. "The guy with his arm around Vera looks like Axel's shaggy-haired partner, before he grew out his hair."

Gray agreed, and Pike handed it off to another officer. "Our friends in Chicago have unearthed a name, and it might belong to Shaggy Hair here. We already knew Axel served one term in the army. Apparently, his closest pal, Milton Byers, enlisted at the same time. They completed basic training together and were both stationed in Fort Campbell. Byers was dishonorably discharged halfway in, and he has failed to recover from that."

They had a disillusioned perp with a grudge against the military on their hands. "Does he have a criminal history?"

"Mostly petty crimes. He served a short stint for assault and battery."

"How did Axel's sidekick meet Vera?" Catriona said. "And how did she get access to that sedative spray?"

"We're running down possible leads on the first issue. As to the spray, Vera is a hospital lab tech. I interviewed her supervisor, and she indicated that Vera is a dependable, hardworking, bright young woman. She's also extremely private."

Catriona twisted the silver ring around her finger. "So no insights into what might've motivated her to steal from her employer and attack a complete stranger."

Gray inventoried the other photographs spread out on Pike's desk. "She was cool under pressure. I will say that. She was determined to accomplish her goal."

"Perhaps she's done side jobs for Byers and Axel in the past."

"Any guesses as to who's running the show?" Gray said.

"Not yet."

"What about the Winthrop compound breach?"

"That's the strange part." Pike's giant glasses slid to the tip of her nose. "According to the guards, Winthrop's personal rooms were targeted. The rest of the mansion was undisturbed. They're inventorying the items."

"They were looking for something," Catriona said. "But what?"

"When we learn more, we'll let you know." She knuckled her glasses into place. "About the safe house… Unfortunately, it's in use. I can appeal to Winthrop and ask if he has any properties in the area."

"Don't bother," Gray said. "He won't help us."

Both women turned questioning gazes on him.

"I submitted my resignation this afternoon."

Catriona gasped. "You didn't tell me."

"I got sidetracked."

Pike snorted. "I'm guessing he didn't take it well."

Catriona touched his arm. "I'm sorry."

"Don't be. I'm committed to bringing Bianca home. After that, I will resume my plans to open my own firm."

Whether clients would request his services after this debacle remained to be seen. That hardly mattered now, with Bianca's life hanging in the balance.

They decided to return to the hotel for the night, then hopefully move on to a new location the following morning. Gray had rented a car because the abductors were familiar with Cat's car. The officer who accompanied them on the return trip would remain at the hotel overnight.

Inside the lobby, Catriona's stride faltered. Gray immediately moved closer to her. She surged forward, however, and was flanked by a man and woman.

"What are you doing here?" Catriona said, clutching the dark-haired woman's hands.

Gray's tension slowly receded. He recognized

her as the one who'd delivered a Bible study workbook to Catriona's home. Olivia, the aquarist.

"Audrey told us you were attacked and brought to the hospital." Olivia's brow was deeply furrowed. "I had to see for myself that you were all right."

"You shouldn't be here," Catriona chided, although her tone seemed to contradict her words.

The tall, commanding man with Olivia settled his hand on Catriona's shoulder. "After everything you've been through, texts and calls weren't enough." His gaze cut into Gray. "You should consider changing up your protective detail. Julian and I can keep you safe."

His message came through loud and clear. Gray stiffened.

Catriona turned toward him and held out her hand. He took it, and she pulled him into their circle.

"You wouldn't say that if you'd seen him in action."

"Oh, yeah?" The blond folded his arms across his chest.

"Yeah," she retorted. "Gray has taken a bullet for me. Dived off a boat and, from what I hear, jumped into a speeding truck to save me."

"Yet you still wound up hurt."

"Enough, Brady." Olivia slipped her arm through his. "Gray, my husband's protective instincts have gone into overdrive since learning he's to become a father. That protection extends to our closest friends. It's not personal."

"I'm grateful Catriona has friends like you who care about her and take her well-being seriously," Gray said.

The officer intervened then and advised them to take their conversation up to the suite. Olivia and Brady joined them there and stayed for more than an hour. As Catriona answered their questions, Gray stood ready to end the visit if she exhibited signs of exhaustion or illness. In his opinion, she hadn't had enough time to recuperate from last night's attack.

When the topic of where they were headed next came up, Olivia and Brady exchanged a look. Gray braced himself. Would they try to convince Catriona to leave his protection and go with them?

"Give me a few hours," Olivia said. "I might be able to help."

Catriona lowered her glass to the counter. "I'm not staying with you."

"I wasn't going to suggest it because I already know your answer."

Brady grunted. "If Julian was here, his solution would be to toss her in the trunk and apologize later."

Gray's breath hissed between his teeth. Catriona covered his hand with her own and smiled at him. "He's joking. Julian would never do that."

"Don't be so sure," Brady replied archly, but humor played about his mouth. His gaze homed in on their joined hands and speculation blossomed.

Catriona yawned. She was too pale for his liking.

"You should get some rest," Gray said softly.

"He's right." Olivia nudged Brady. "Time to go."

"Already?"

She leaned into him and patted her swollen abdomen. "The baby is craving chocolate chip ice cream."

His expression softening, he curled his arm around her. "I happen to know of an ice cream shop nearby. I think you've been there before."

"Once or twice." She chuckled.

"Don't deny that the employees know your name and usual order." Catriona joined in the teasing.

Olivia rested her hand on his chest. "I blame him." To Gray, she said, "Brady has a love affair with dairy."

Catriona agreed. "You should see his freezer. I counted ten different kinds last time I was there."

Brady wagged his finger. "Don't be spilling my secrets, Sergeant."

They got ready to leave and took turns hugging her. Gray stood off to the side. It was good to see her with her friends, good to know she wouldn't be alone once this was over. Once he'd left North Carolina.

The thought soured his mood.

Before they walked out the door, Brady turned to Gray and extended his hand for a shake. "I trust you'll keep her safe," he said gruffly.

"I'll do whatever I have to do."

"That's what I want to hear."

The door closed behind them. Catriona crossed to stand before him. "You'll do whatever you have to do without putting yourself at further risk, you mean."

He met her stare without speaking.

"Gray—"

He cupped her cheek. "Don't ask the impossible, Catriona."

NINETEEN

Cat's restlessness that night had nothing to do with her new, unfamiliar surroundings. Olivia had come through for them. One of her coworkers, who was out of town on aquarium business, had agreed to let Cat and Gray stay in his home. Shane lived in a quiet, older neighborhood in the heart of Jacksonville. They'd packed their stuff and driven here under cover of darkness. Axel and his cohorts wouldn't be able to link them to the aquarium or Shane.

Cat tiptoed into the kitchen. There was a rustling on the couch, and she heard Gray sit up and slip on his shoes. Not a single light illuminated the home's interior.

"Can't sleep?" His voice was rough, and she could imagine him running his hands through his dark waves.

"Can't get my mind to settle," she said, turning on the under-the-cabinet lights. "I'm sorry I disturbed you."

Gray joined her. Muted light washed over his pronounced cheekbones, chiseled jaw and sculpted mouth. "I was dozing, that's all."

"I keep thinking about Pike's news."

She'd called before they left the hotel and told them Vera's body had been discovered in the woods near her home.

Gray's expression was grim. "I wasn't expecting that outcome."

The ruthless act troubled Cat.

Too keyed up to relax, she made coffee. "The photograph of Vera with Milton Byers, if that is his name, is an older one. They've been together a while. Would he kill her simply to ensure her silence?"

"Maybe he wasn't involved. The order could've come from the one in charge, and some other goon carried it out." Gray searched the cabinets and located two mugs. "We have no idea how many we're dealing with."

"Today marks a week since Bianca was taken. These people have the means and skills to hide her well. They haven't wavered in their mission to abduct me, despite being unsuccessful to this point."

"Greed and arrogance have brought down many a criminal mastermind. They'll get tired and desperate, which will lead to mistakes."

Tired and desperate meant short fuses.

"Would you like to pray together?" he said.

Cat thought of the verse Olivia often quoted. *For where two or more are gathered together in my name, I am there in the midst of them.*

"I'd like that."

Gray's prayer was natural and intimate. Cat stumbled through hers, but she experienced renewed confidence. God wouldn't abandon her. He wouldn't abandon Bianca, either.

They also prayed for Vera's loved ones, who would soon learn of their loss. They sipped their decaf in companionable silence, and eventually Gray decided to get some sleep. He encouraged her to try, as well. Who knew what the following hours would bring?

She tossed and turned until dawn before giving up and returning to the kitchen to make fresh coffee—full strength this time. She surveyed the street and was surprised to see an unfamiliar car in the driveway. Officer Dunham, who'd taken the night shift, was conversing with the driver.

"What are you looking at?"

She pressed her hand to her chest. "You startled me."

Gray was at her elbow, his hair as unruly as ever and his jaw shadowed with scruff. "Sorry."

"Looks like we have a visitor. Dunham's grilling him." Together they watched as the driver emerged. He looked to be college age and had short dark hair.

Beside her, Gray expelled a sharp burst of air. "Ryan."

He was out the door before she could question him. Cat trailed him as far as the stoop. Gray hesitated at the last second, uncertainty stamped on his face. Ryan reached in for a hug. When they parted, both men were grinning from ear to ear, and she saw the unmistakable resemblance.

Ryan Michaelson was a younger, lankier version of his older brother.

"When I texted you our new location last night, I didn't expect you to show up." Gray's voice carried as they approached.

"I had to see you in person, to make sure you're okay."

They joined her on the stoop, and Ryan oozed curiosity.

"Ryan, I'd like you to meet Sergeant Catriona Baker."

She was suddenly self-conscious. What would Gray's brother make of her? Would he detect her growing feelings for Gray? Would Ryan warn him to stay away from someone like her?

Ryan gifted her with a charming grin. "It's nice to finally meet you, Catriona. You're even lovelier in person than on video chat. My brother is a fortunate man."

"Fortunate? Since setting foot in North Carolina, he's gotten attacked, shot at and chased."

"You forgot the homemade pipe bombs," Gray dryly quipped.

"Yes, but he had you by his side."

Everything about his brother was familiar. The way he slouched in a chair, his outburst of laughter, his outrageous teasing. Gray felt a welling of affection for the young man.

Over breakfast the three of them had prepared together, Ryan regaled them with tales of their childhood. Gray was painted as both a bossy dictator and a staunch protector.

"You know I'll verify these stories with Fallon."

Ryan's eyes sparkled over the rim of his juice glass. He refused to drink coffee like a rational adult. "What kind of person do you think I am? I wouldn't lie to an amnesiac."

Gray turned his head to look at Catriona, seated beside him. She'd lost the wariness that had characterized her expression in recent days. Her mouth was curved in amusement, and her eyes were full and bright. If Ryan wasn't acting as a chaperone, he would've kissed her.

"What's your take, Catriona? Should we believe him?"

She cocked her head to one side. "I say we give him the benefit of the doubt."

Ryan pumped his fist.

Catriona chuckled. "I'd love to hear more, but I'm going to take a nap."

He told her that he and Ryan would clean up. She smiled sweetly, thanked him and retreated to her bedroom.

Gray didn't know if she liked to take naps or if she was intentionally giving them time alone. He knew she was gutsy and competent, vulnerable and lonely. He wanted to know more, like what stamps she wanted on her passport and what her best day looked like.

A low whistle diverted the direction of his thoughts. "You've got it bad, big brother."

The grin was in place, but Ryan's gaze had turned serious.

Gray propped his arm atop the chair she'd vacated. "That's quite a pronouncement after one meal."

"My memories of you are fully intact. I've seen you serious about only one other woman, and this feels different." He paused. "I don't have to spend any more time with Catriona to know *she's* different."

"Since I'm clearly at a disadvantage, I'm not having this conversation with you."

Gray pushed his chair out and began to stack dishes.

"Fallon's the one with the preference for redheads," Ryan said slyly. "Maybe you could introduce them."

He gritted his teeth and marched to the sink.

Ryan followed with silverware and rested his

hip against the counter. "She is closer to our age. I'll ask her to take a picture with me before I go, and then message it to him. Or maybe she'd agree to start up an online friendship. You never know—"

"Enough." Gray shut off the water. "I know what you're trying to do."

"Is it working?"

He scraped the sponge across the soiled dishes with more force than necessary. "It's complicated."

"What's standing in your way?"

"The fact I'm operating with an incomplete puzzle, not to mention I live multiple states away." There was the age difference, too, although she didn't seem to mind.

"You have to ask yourself what's more important. A place or a person?" He shrugged. "It's a no-brainer."

The words thrust him into another time and place. Images passed through his mind. Ryan trying to convince him that Angel didn't have his best interests at heart. Ryan goading him off the couch and into daily life again after his injury had ended his career.

"I get along with you better than I do with Fallon. Why?"

"You two are cut from the same cloth."

"Can you be more specific?"

"You take life too seriously."

Gray crossed his arms and stared at him.

"You're both highly driven individuals. You don't like to fail. Those high expectations lead to competition, which I happen to think is healthy. Mom doesn't agree."

Gray processed the statement. It felt right. When this was over, he'd make plans to fly to Germany and speak to Fallon face-to-face.

Ryan lingered until after lunch. Catriona joined them for sandwiches, and once again, his little brother turned on the charm. Gray would've liked to extend their time together, but it wasn't the safest place for him.

Gray followed him to his car, where Ryan dropped the teasing routine. "Gray, listen to me. Your memories aren't fully restored yet, but you haven't changed. You're the same guy I grew up wanting to emulate. If you care about her, you have to fight for her."

Not giving him a chance to respond, Ryan hugged him, climbed into his vehicle and reversed out of the driveway. Gray was sorry to see him go. Maybe Ryan could manage some vacation time and fly to Germany with him.

A text from Pike came through. His blood ran cold.

There's been a development. Watch the local news.

Was it Bianca? Had they arrested Axel?
He went inside and knew immediately the news

was bad. Catriona was staring, shell-shocked, at the television above the fireplace.

The news montage featured images of both Winthrop and Catriona.

"Business tycoon Wayne Winthrop has claimed US Marine Sergeant Catriona Baker is not his daughter. However, leaked DNA results allege otherwise." The anchor turned to her partner. "Dale, do we know who's behind the leak?"

"From all accounts, the criminal group responsible for taking Bianca Winthrop hostage is the source."

Gray found the remote lodged into the cushions and muted the commentary. "This could be a stunt."

"After the park bombings, we returned to the cottage and found the door ajar. No one was there to ambush us, and nothing was missing. The same scenario played out at the Winthrop compound. Of course, we wouldn't notice if personal items were taken. Things like toothbrushes or used dental floss."

Gray settled his hands on her shoulders. "We'll get to the bottom of this, I promise."

"What if it's true?" she whispered. "What if that hateful man is my father?"

TWENTY

Over the course of her life, Cat had weathered nasty shocks and disappointments. None compared with this one. If the DNA test was valid, her own father had forced her mother to give her up for adoption. He'd seen to it that she'd grown up apart from her flesh-and-blood family.

Her phone vibrated for the fifth time in as many minutes. Gray placed a tray on the coffee table and answered it for her.

"She doesn't want to talk to you, Winthrop." He ended the call without waiting for a response.

Sitting beside her, he waved his hand over the tray contents as if he were a game show host.

"I raided the cabinets and freezer," he said. "Don't worry. I'll leave extra cash for Shane. What do you want first? Chocolate peanut butter candies, sandwich cookies, strawberry licorice ropes or chemically colored fruit pops?" He picked up a foil bag. "I also found cheddar popcorn. It's past the expiration date, but some people aren't bothered by that."

Cat's gaze bounced between him and the sugar buffet; she wasn't sure whether to laugh or cry.

His concern deepened to consternation. "You don't like any of this. Tell me your favorite comfort food snack, and I'll go get it. Better yet, I'll text Pike a list."

Cat leaned forward, braced her weight against his strong shoulder and kissed his cheek. Resuming her spot, she saw him blink.

"What was that for?"

"I'm glad you're here with me, Gray."

He put the popcorn back and got comfortable on the couch. Only one cushion separated them. His body was angled toward her, his eyes begging the question—*What can I do to make things better?*

He held out his hand, and she linked her fingers with his.

"Winthrop isn't going to go away," he said.

"I will listen to what he has to say, when I'm ready."

"The DNA test was performed using unusual samples like the ones you mentioned. Pike will want you and Winthrop to give known samples so the department can perform their own test."

"This is going to intensify the scrutiny on my life." She traced the pale veins on his hand and learned his palm was ticklish. "I'm surprised they haven't unearthed my sordid 'infatuation' with Sergeant Craft."

"When and if they do, we'll face it together."

There was no one besides Gray that she would want to weather the approaching storms with. Friend, teammate, companion, romantic ideal... He was each of those things to her. How he felt about her was a mystery.

"This could mean that my whole life, I have had a mother, father and sister. We lived in the same city, even."

"Hermione said Wayne and Tabitha had trouble conceiving. The timing of her affair must've been such that he assumed the other man was the father."

"Even if Tabitha had suspected, he wouldn't have listened to her." She ripped open the licorice bag. "Maybe this will galvanize Winthrop into being more cooperative with the police. Pike hasn't uncovered any suspects connected to Bianca's life. We have to entertain the possibility that the people behind this are tied to his business activities."

"You could be the one to facilitate that," he suggested softly.

"Meet with him in exchange for his sitting down with Pike and giving her full access to his life."

"I'd be with you the entire time."

What could one conversation hurt? "Hand me the phone."

She texted Wayne her demands—one meeting with her meant he'd play nice with the authorities. He quickly acquiesced.

"He's rented office space in a building on Western Avenue. He'll have his security team in place." Her heart thumped out an uneasy rhythm. "We rendezvous in two hours."

The designated office building was tucked into a complex of big-box stores and restaurants. Dunham had followed them and agreed to keep watch outside until Pike arrived. From the top-floor boardroom where Winthrop's guards had kept them waiting, they had an unobstructed view of the traveling carnival. The Ferris wheel and other rides occupied the large parking area between this building and the movie theater.

A brilliant blue sky set the backdrop for the kaleidoscope of garish greens, yellows and pinks. Triangular flags rippled in the wind. Fairgoers clogged the pavement aisles, eager to spend their cash on fried foods and stuffed animals too large for their cars.

Catriona walked a circuitous path on the patterned carpet, her jaw clenched and lips pursed. Her outfit, a sleeveless lilac blouse paired with white shorts and white tennis shoes, showcased her toned, feminine physique. She'd restrained her flame-red hair with a sparkly band, then twisted it into a long, shining tail. Her beauty and strength amazed him. He longed to intercept her, frame her face with his hands and chase away the tension with a lingering kiss.

The door at the far end of the room opened, and she squared her shoulders and turned to face Winthrop.

His lack of composure stunned Gray. The suit was clean and pressed, the tie expertly situated and shoes shined to perfection. That was where the claim to calm ended. Winthrop's features were aged with a straggly beard. His hair had lost its salon freshness, and his eyes were bloodshot.

"Mr. Michaelson. Catriona." His throat worked as he gazed at her. "Thank you for agreeing to meet with me."

"I'm here because of Bianca."

"Yes, of course." He glanced at his guards. "Wait outside."

Winthrop approached Catriona, who stood her ground and met his gaze head-on.

"The first time I saw you, I was bowled over by your resemblance to Tabitha. Now that I know you're my daughter, I can see something of my mother in you."

"We won't know that for sure until an official test is performed."

"There's no doubt in my mind. I've done my research, Catriona. You've thrived in difficult circumstances. You've shown grit in the face of adversity. You're a Winthrop, all right." He held out a card. "I've arranged for you to go out of state, to a friend's home. No one will find you there."

Catriona's jaw dropped. "You tossed me to the wolves when you thought I didn't possess the coveted Winthrop pedigree. Excuse me if I don't buy the protective daddy routine."

He hunched forward. "I'm sorry about that. I was desperate. I still am, truth be told. Desperate to rescue Bianca and to keep my newly discovered daughter safe."

"How do you sleep at night?" She was trembling. "My heritage aside, you bullied your wife into giving up her baby."

He flushed. "Tabitha and I both made mistakes."

Catriona didn't immediately respond, and Gray decided to intervene.

"Once we have Bianca home again, the three of you can decide if you want to spend time together."

"I'd like that," Winthrop said. "What about you, Catriona?"

"I'm not committing to anything. I'm not going to your friend's, either."

"But—"

The shriek of a fire alarm pulsed through the building, and Winthrop's guards rushed inside. They hustled him out before he could offer up much of a protest. Gray and Catriona followed them into the stairwell. Although it was Saturday, some of the companies were open for business, and employees streamed in from each floor.

The air didn't reek of smoke. The chatter around him led Gray to believe there was no active fire. It was also unlikely that this was a prank perpetrated by a bored teenager, not when there was an amusement park to occupy their time. Outside in the midafternoon sunshine, fire trucks screamed into the complex. Pike hadn't made an appearance, which left Dunham to corral the growing number of employees wondering where to go.

Catriona pulled him aside. "Do we go straight to our vehicle and take the chance someone is watching?"

It wouldn't be the first time Axel and his crew had followed Winthrop.

"Let's take a detour through the carnival."

"Will you buy me cotton candy and popcorn?"

"I'll even toss in a corn dog."

The smell of fried sausages, onions and peppers dominated the side entrance area, and Gray's stomach rumbled in response. Ignoring the hunger pangs, he navigated the narrow walkways, alert to any hint of danger. This was a security nightmare...exposed on all sides, unlimited places for a criminal to hide, distractions competing for his attention.

"Let's use the next exit we come to and walk the perimeter."

Catriona's gaze lingered on the parents with young children. "Kurt and Dana brought me to a fair once."

The swings geared up for another go, and the grinding gears and riders' yelps of delight prevented her from speaking.

Several booths down, she continued. "That day ranks as one of my best childhood memories. Their biological kids were spending that Saturday with friends, and I was over the moon at having them all to myself." Her smile was wistful. "I can't help wondering how different my life would've been had Tabitha defied Wayne's wishes."

"I guarantee you wouldn't have been allowed to visit a lowly fair. That's for commoners." He winked at her.

"Or eat junk food," she said. "I probably wouldn't have joined the Marines, and that makes me sad."

"That makes *me* sad. You're an asset to our nation's fighting force."

She blushed. "Thank you, Gray."

They reached the end of that row, and he considered leaving by unconventional means. They'd have to squeeze between tents and would likely earn the ire of fair workers. He asked the fresh-squeezed-lemonade lady where to find the next best exit. Following her convoluted directions, they wound through another aisle of attractions.

Near the hall of mirrors, they encountered a group of kindergartners. The thirty or so kids, plus their chaperones, swelled through the space wielding dripping ice cream cones. Amid the happy chaos, his path was blocked by a double stroller being pushed by an expectant mother. The wheel became stuck, and he bent to unwind the diaper bag strap. When he finished, Catriona was nowhere to be seen.

Dread curling behind his sternum, he completed a full circle, scanning the booths and crowd for her.

She wouldn't leave him, not of her own volition.

He searched again, up and down the parade of tents, his thin veneer of calm crumbling.

She was in trouble, and he had to help her. But he had to find her first.

TWENTY-ONE

"Catriona?"

Two long strides away, partially hidden by a dumbbell-wielding plywood caricature, stood her sister.

"Bianca?"

In no way did this young woman match the online images. Her long hair was lank and dull, the ends tangled. Dirt was embedded in her hairline, and there were dark smudges on her neck. Her clothes were two sizes too big and clearly borrowed. But to Cat, she was the most beautiful sight in the world.

Bianca was alive and well.

The shock and joy muted her well-honed instincts. It didn't even occur to Cat that her sudden appearance was suspect.

Closing the distance between them, she gripped her hand. "You're okay."

Her lower lip trembled, and tears coursed down her cheeks. "I'm sorry."

Out of the tent's shadows, Axel emerged and jammed a gun to Bianca's ribs.

"Let's take a walk."

Right. This wasn't a happy reunion. After all, how could a young woman with no tactical training escape her armed and dangerous captors and find her way to this exact spot?

"Put on your sunglasses," he spit, and Bianca lifted a large black pair and slid them on.

Axel then dropped a wide-brimmed hat on Bianca's head.

Cat held tightly to Bianca's hand as they shuffled toward the exit. The girl was visibly shaking. Was she ill? Malnourished?

"I'm sorry," she said again. "They threatened to kill my father if I didn't—"

"Shut up."

Axel must've jammed the gun deeper into her side, because Bianca winced and stumbled. He grabbed her arm in a punishing grip and growled something ugly in her ear.

Fury suffused Cat until she herself was trembling. She'd had enough of these bullies.

Escape was the only option. They were surrounded by innocent people, many of them children, which limited her choices. She couldn't put them in danger. Couldn't put Gray at risk, either. He wouldn't stop searching for her until he'd combed every inch of the fairgrounds.

Corralling her anger, she put it to work. Her vision became sharper, her hearing more attuned to their surroundings. What Axel didn't know was that her loose-fitting blouse hid her Glock. She had to bide her time, that was all.

As they neared the exit, she realized the white van was waiting for them. They'd chosen this spot because several pines and oaks provided a natural barrier between the van and nearby stands.

No good. Her steps slowed.

Once inside that van, they were beyond help.

She glanced around. An older couple shared a treat on a bench beneath the trees. A lone teenager scrolled through his phone over by the smoothie vendor.

The side van door slid open.

Bianca's shaking intensified.

Cat was not going to allow those thugs to gain control of her again.

Taking a bracing breath, she threw all her weight into Axel. She ordered Bianca to run. His arm snaked around Cat's neck and squeezed.

Cat brought her heel up between his legs, striking him in the groin, and dropped down to the ground, forcing him to release her.

Before he could recover, she rolled to a crouch and went for him again, managing to knock the gun from his grasp.

Out of the corner of her eye, she noticed Bianca hadn't moved an inch. Cat grabbed her hand and tugged.

"Come on!" Together, they zigzagged through the stunned crowd. "This way!"

Cat led her around a spinning carousel, not daring to look back. She didn't have time to get a call out to Gray. They bumped into a pair of women, and popcorn went flying.

"He's coming," Bianca gasped, her eyes wide with fright.

Grasping Bianca's hand more firmly, Cat plunged them into connecting tents supplied with chairs and tables, most likely a break area for the carnival workers. Picking up the flap, she urged Bianca through. On the other side, the door to a storage shed stood wide open.

"In here."

Bianca balked, but Cat guided her in and pulled the creaking door closed. Darkness cloaked them. The temperature inside the metal structure was hot enough to fry an egg. Sweat trickled beneath her collar.

"What if he finds us?" she cried. "I can't go back there—"

Pounding steps on the concrete outside threatened their hiding spot. Cat removed her weapon and released the safety. Whoever was out there suddenly stopped.

A protesting moan bubbled up inside Bianca. Cat shifted in front of her.

The door was yanked open, and Cat wielded her weapon, her finger on the trigger.

"Gray!" Bianca flew into his arms.

Gray stumbled a step back. Lowering his weapon, he awkwardly patted her shoulder and locked gazes with Cat.

"I almost shot you," she said, adrenaline causing a jittery aftershock.

"I'm grateful you didn't," he returned.

Bianca lifted her head. "I thought you were dead, like poor Ross." Fresh tears welled. "I'm sorry I got you involved in this. You should've let me come alone."

He got a perplexed, almost pained look. She recognized it as a sign he was remembering something.

"You told me I wasn't needed at the mall," he said, his eyes glazing over. "You'd already arranged for Ross to go, which was a red flag. It was no secret that you had Ross wrapped around your finger and that he'd agree to almost any request."

Her brow knit. "Why are you talking like that?"

He pinched the bridge of his nose.

She turned an alarmed gaze on Cat. "What's wrong with him?"

"That first night, he suffered a head injury and lost his memories."

She covered her mouth with her hand. Her nails were broken and dirty, and her wrists were rubbed raw from being restrained.

"He followed us to the mall," she said, her

words muffled. "When I tried to slip away without Ross, Gray intercepted me and insisted I confess my plans. He thought I was planning to run away with Lane, my boyfriend."

"Instead, this fantastical story spilled out," Gray uttered with painstaking slowness. "About a journal and a long-lost sister—"

"You didn't believe me," Bianca interrupted softly. "You thought it was a product of my grief."

He looked at Cat. "Then I saw the photo of you, and I couldn't deny the family resemblance. I kept it in my wallet as a reminder we were doing the right thing leaving Chicago and coming on this quest."

His blue eyes had cleared. There was something different. Awareness. Understanding.

"You remember."

He swallowed hard. "I remember."

Her heart leaped. "Everything?"

"Not everything. When I saw Bianca, some major puzzle pieces snapped into place."

There was no time to celebrate or give thanks to God. Axel and his thugs were still out there, hunting them.

"We have to get Bianca to the police station," she said. "It's the only place she'll be safe."

"Who's behind this, Bianca?" Gray whipped the rental car out of the complex and onto the main thoroughfare.

"I haven't met the one in charge." She lifted her hand to her mouth in order to bite her nails and thought better of it. "I've heard him speak to Axel. He sounds familiar. I've tried to place him, but I can't."

"Have they been giving you food and water?" Cat had crawled into the back with Bianca. She knew she was staring, but she couldn't stop herself.

Bianca knotted her hands in her lap. "Twice a day. Mostly junk food."

"Have they mistreated you?"

She lifted her chin, but there was a telltale wobble. "Nothing I couldn't handle."

Cat tapped Gray's shoulder. "Should we go to the hospital first and have Pike meet us there?"

"I don't need a doctor." Her eyes were the exact combination of silver green Cat had seen in the mirror her whole life. "This is nothing like how I imagined our first meeting going."

There were so many questions. What to ask first? "How did you learn of Tabitha's first pregnancy?"

"I put off going through my mother's personal things for months. When I finally did, I found old letters she'd written to her friend Hermione."

"We met her."

"You did?"

"She lives about an hour south. She clearly adored your mom." *Our* mom.

"I spoke with her on the phone," Bianca said, "and that conversation convinced me to hire an investigator."

Gray huffed from the front seat. "I don't know how I missed that."

A tiny smile flashed. "After four years, I've learned how to keep certain things hidden from you."

In the rearview mirror, he arched a brow. "I'll have to change up my procedures." He paused, no doubt remembering he no longer worked for the Winthrops.

"It took several months of circumventing road-blocks, but the investigator finally located the retired social worker who handled Catriona's case. From there, he followed the trail to the New River Air Station Base." She smiled at Catriona. "My sister, a US marine. Imagine that. Could I— Can I give you a hug?"

Cat's throat grew thick. At her nod, Bianca wrapped her arms around her shoulders. A tremor passed through her too-thin frame. Cat held her close, despite her not-so-fresh smell.

Lord Jesus, thank You. Thank You for hearing my heart's cry and bringing about the reunion of a lifetime.

Cat didn't need official tests to prove they were sisters. She felt the connection in her soul.

When they separated, Cat gingerly pushed a stray strand out of Bianca's eyes. "We need your help locating these guys. What can you tell us about where they held you?"

A shadow passed over her face. "I had a blindfold on. Once inside my room, I was allowed to take it off. Brick walls, no windows."

"What did it smell like? Did you hear anything?"

"Like dirt and dust. It was quiet when they led me inside that first night. No traffic or city noise. Sometimes I'd hear strange revving sounds."

Gray executed a right turn near the hospital. They would reach the station soon.

"Anything else?"

She closed her eyes. "Once, when they delivered food, I glimpsed part of a hallway. The floor was a light-colored tile, old and chipped."

Cat met Gray's gaze in the mirror. There wasn't much to go on, but it was a start.

"How's my father? Have you spoken to him? He must be furious with me."

Cat considered telling Bianca everything, specifically that Wayne Winthrop was in all likelihood her father, too. It could wait until she had a chance to clean up, eat a nice, healthy meal and rest.

Gray shook his head. "He's not angry with you, B. He's focused solely on bringing you home."

Cat noticed a truck hurtling down a side street. "Gray—"

"I see it."

He yanked the wheel hard to the right. The truck barreled through the stop sign. Its massive grille with protruding guards bore down on them. Gray stomped on the gas. It wasn't enough to avoid the collision.

The truck slammed into the rear wheel well. The car rocked and spun, the screech of crunching metal assaulting their ears. Another jolt rattled the vehicle—they'd rammed into an official post office mail receptacle that accordioned the trunk. The jarring force deployed Gray's airbag. In seconds, armed men were upon them, throwing open the doors and pulling Bianca and Cat out.

Bianca's screams turned her blood cold. The truck loomed nearby, engine humming, Axel at the wheel. A sports car approached, music blaring, then slammed on the brakes and quickly reversed.

Cat bucked the blond stranger's efforts to propel her closer. Ahead, the skinny man she'd twice encountered was wrestling to control an uncooperative Bianca.

Gray extricated himself from the airbag and, using the door for cover, aimed his weapon. The skinny man ignored his shouted warning.

Cat seized the opportunity to launch an offense. She managed to free herself and fight the blond goon off long enough to draw her weapon. He fingered his own, giving her no choice but to fire. The bullet dug into his thigh, bringing him to his knees. She relieved him of his gun and tossed it in the field.

Whirling about, she saw the gun pointed at Bianca's head.

"Let her go," she implored, desperation leaking into her voice.

Bianca's face had lost all color, and her anguish-filled eyes begged Cat to stop this.

Gray eased from behind the door, his gun outstretched. Sirens whirred in the distance.

"The authorities are en route," Gray said. "Leave the girl and make your escape."

From inside the vehicle, Axel issued a command. The skinny man was positioned behind Bianca. Cat couldn't get a clear shot. He took a step back, compelling Bianca to do the same.

Then he pointed his gun at them and pulled the trigger. They dived to the ground.

The truck roared away with Bianca inside. They'd taken her and left one of their own.

"No!"

Cat scrabbled to her feet and raced after them, unwilling to accept she'd found her sister and lost her again. She ignored Gray's calls to stop. She pushed her legs to carry her faster, to take longer strides. The truck was getting smaller, the distance between them too great to cross.

When her defiant mind accepted that her efforts were futile, she slowed and fell to her knees in the middle of the road.

TWENTY-TWO

Catriona's utter dejection practically ripped Gray's heart from his chest. When he went to wrap his arms around her, she shoved him away.

"Don't." She gulped in great gasps of air, and he suspected she was on the verge of a panic attack. There were no tears. Not yet. Her pale, drawn features bore testament to her iron grip on her emotions.

The sirens grew louder. He glanced again at the downed man, who, though conscious, was unable to walk.

"I got a license plate number," Gray told her. "We have one of their men."

Avoiding his outstretched hand, she lumbered to her feet and retraced her steps.

"Where are they taking her?" she demanded.

The blond lifted his hateful gaze and sneered. "You'll join her soon enough."

Gray snagged her arm when she started to lunge for the wounded man.

"Let the officers do their job." He nodded to the pair of patrol cars almost upon them.

He knew from experience that the chances of the man offering up valuable intel were slim. He knew because his memories had been almost fully restored. There were less fuzzy gaps and fewer unanswered questions, and for that he praised God.

Shaking off his hand, Catriona flashed her military ID and quickly informed the officers. Gray relayed the plate numbers, and she led them to the discarded weapon.

"You won't let them get away, right?" Catriona challenged. "They have maybe a five-minute head start."

"We have units searching for them, ma'am."

The evasive response further frustrated Catriona. She stalked away. An ambulance arrived and took the perp for treatment. Once they'd given their statements, Catriona insisted on returning to Shane's. As they retrieved her Chevelle and made the trip unescorted, she didn't speak a word.

Gray didn't press her. He was sorting through his own too-big emotions.

They swept the house together.

"All clear," he said, returning his weapon to his holster. He watched her stalk to the living room window, grip the painted sill and stare at the street. Her forlorn, solitary pose gutted him.

She didn't have to endure this alone, yet that was her default.

He approached her as he would a flight risk. "What do you need right now, Catriona? Comfort food? Mindless television? Card game?"

"Privacy." Not meeting his gaze, she pivoted and brushed past him. The door to her room slammed shut.

He fisted his hands, bowed his head and asked God for wisdom. In the silence, he heard the tell-tale slide of glass. Gray exited via the front door, walked around the house and entered the secluded backyard through a wooden gate. Tall, thick uniform bushes formed an impenetrable barrier between this yard and the neighbors'. He nearly collided with Catriona.

"Where are you going?"

She glared at him. "Get out of my way, Michaelson."

"Oh, we're back to formalities, are we? Sergeant Baker, do you mind telling me why you're sneaking out in broad daylight?"

"I don't have to tell you anything." She started to sidestep him, and he mirrored her move, holding out his hands.

"You think I'm not sick with worry about her?" he said. "That I don't blame myself?"

She sucked in a sharp breath, and her face spasmed with grief. "There's no time to dwell on our inadequacies. Don't you get that? We have to do everything we can to find her!"

"That night in the park, I should've been more aware of the threat. Protecting her is what I do, what I've done for four years. I don't know if it was being out of Chicago that made me careless or if I was distracted by Bianca's giddy enthusiasm. You should've seen her. She was like a little girl on Christmas morning. After the hard year of grieving her mom, she'd finally come alive again."

Catriona pressed her hand to her stomach.

"I saw the car roll in," he said, pained at the memory of how he'd botched things. "I didn't assess the threat potential. I assumed they were bored teenagers. Because of me, Ross is dead and Bianca is a hostage."

She shook her head. "You want to know where I'm going? To the station. To drive the city streets. I'm going to search until I find something that will lead us to her."

They both needed to wade through the pain. Ignoring it, allowing it to fester, would lead to costly mistakes. "Today I was distracted again. At the fairgrounds and again in the car. Seeing the two of you together—" He took a breath. "There was no denying the instant bond you shared."

"Stop." The command was more of a moan.

"I was mesmerized. This girl that I've guarded and watched grow into a special young woman had found the big sister of her dreams. You're an unexpected link to the mother and best friend she lost too soon. And then there was you." His heart thundered in his chest. "This brave, competent, amazing woman who'd soldiered through life without the benefit of a family had discovered that she wasn't alone after all. I could hardly keep my eyes on the road."

A soft wailing sound escaped her, and she hunched over. Sobs racked her frame.

Gray cupped her upper arms and pulled her into his embrace. She started to resist, to fight him.

"Trust me, Cat."

"No." The word was more of a plea than a denial.

Before his past had come rushing back, he'd acknowledged Catriona was special. Now he understood the depth of his feelings. Although they couldn't be together—she was a blue-blood heiress and he the hired help—he could be her friend.

"I can take it all. Your pain, your anger and disillusionment. Your sorrow. All of it."

Her hands fisted in his shirt, and she collapsed against him, weeping.

Gray traced circles on her quivering back and prayed. While he could offer physical comfort, God could heal her brokenness and restore peace to her weary heart.

Help me, Father. I'm a selfish man, and I would like nothing better than to have a future with Catriona. Help me to want what's best for her.

Her tears gradually subsided, and he led her inside the house and to the master bathroom, where she made use of the tissue box. He wet a washcloth and carefully washed her sorrow-ravaged face.

Seated on the sink counter, her hands curled around the edge, she was quiet yet watchful.

Gray looped the cloth over the faucet. "Are you hungry? Thirsty?"

Reaching out, she snagged his wrist. Her eyes were as luminous as the constellations. "I hate the circumstances that brought us together, but I will never regret knowing you."

His mouth went dry. He yearned to repeat their previous kiss, but that prayer...

Catriona shifted to the counter's edge and tugged him closer, her gaze zeroing in on his mouth. His thoughts splintered, and he cupped her silken cheek. "You take my breath away," he whispered.

Her cheeks bloomed with color. Releasing his hand, she twined her arms around his neck and lifted her face to his. Her lips were soft and inviting. She delved her fingers into his hair and explored the too-long waves. His pulse raced, his heart tripped over itself, and he knew he'd never felt this way about anyone else and never would.

Cat was journeying deeper and deeper into unmapped territory.

Gray had broken through a barrier, and she'd

let him. Being vulnerable with him was new and frightening but comforting in a strange way. She'd leaned on him, physically and emotionally, and she wasn't resistant to doing it again.

Beneath her hand, beneath his sturdy, warm chest, beat a trustworthy heart. A mighty warrior's heart that was coming to mean a great deal to her. If he were to leave—

What do you mean if? her mind warned. *When he leaves, you'll be alone again. Hurting and lonely, the blackest-night loneliness that cripples you.*

But who else would've ministered to her so tenderly?

Gray's kisses made her wish forever was possible.

She pushed against his chest, and he lifted his head and took a step back. His eyes were heavy-lidded and his hair in disarray. He was magnificent in every way, and he was out of her reach.

Hopping off the counter, she left the master suite. He followed her to the living room.

"What happened at the park wasn't your fault," she told him, taking up position at the window. "Neither was today. We were both understandably overwhelmed. Instead of dwelling on what we can't change, let's work toward finding her."

He rested his hands on the side chair and contemplated her for long moments.

Please don't insist on analyzing that kiss, she

silently implored. What would it achieve besides reminding them both it had been a mistake?

"We could go talk to Pike," he finally said. "Look through Vera's photos and other belongings again."

It would probably be an exercise in futility. His tone and gaze conveyed his doubts. But she couldn't just sit here and do nothing.

They locked up the house and headed to the station. Cat studied the darkening streets outside her window, desperate for a sighting of the truck, even though she knew it was unlikely. They rolled through an intersection. Her gaze swept over a popular barbecue restaurant. Inside, diners crowded the eating area, and there was a line at the counter. As they drove past the building, she shot up in her seat. "Turn here."

He quickly heeded her command. "What did you see?"

She pointed to an older-model van parked in the back. "The van we saw in Wilmington and at the fairgrounds had the faded letters *ATE* on the side. We couldn't see the rest of the words. The make and model are the same."

He turned into the parking lot and pulled alongside it. "'RAY'S BARBECUE CATERING.'" His eyes gleamed with renewed purpose. "Let's have a chat with the owner."

TWENTY-THREE

"The van's mine." Ray Griffin, the owner of the city's most popular barbecue chain, studied the photograph. "I purchased three new vans about six weeks ago and put For Sale signs on the old ones. The first one went in a day. I had trouble finding buyers for the others. Last Saturday, I arrived for work and noticed one was missing."

"Did you report it?" Officer Wong asked. The officer had met them at the restaurant and promised to brief Pike when she was available.

"Nah." He gestured to the redbrick building behind him. "We don't have security cameras. I figured the police wouldn't put much effort into finding the culprits. It was valued at one thousand dollars."

The lack of cameras was a disappointment. Gray studied the surroundings again. The restaurant was located on a busy Jacksonville artery. A narrow street leading into a neighborhood ran along one side. A tire company occupied that street-front lot. Across the main road, there was a strip mall.

Catriona tapped the photo. "Do you recognize either one of these people?"

"I have plenty of regulars. This couple doesn't look familiar."

The van, along with Ray's new ones, was parked near the small buildings that housed his meat smokers.

Catriona gestured to the bank. "Gray, look."

The bank's drive-through and ATM faced the restaurant. He consulted his watch. "They're closed."

"Now, why didn't I think of that?" Ray harrumphed. "I know the bank manager. Let me give him a call."

Hope sparked in her eyes. "We'd appreciate it."

"I've been following the media coverage. If I can help bring that young woman home, I will."

Gray, Catriona and Officer Wong couldn't help but overhear Ray's phone conversation. He explained about the robbery and the role it might play in Bianca's abduction. The bank manager, Tom Reiss, agreed to return to the bank and show them the security video footage.

While they waited, Ray plied them with barbecue sandwiches and sweet tea. Catriona faked enthusiasm for the older man's sake. She'd regained her composure in the hours since their run-in with Axel and his crew, but she was different from before. There was a brittleness to her, a suggestion that she wasn't invincible. Meeting her sister had made this ordeal more trying.

Mr. Reiss met them at the bank after a forty-five-minute wait. He chatted with Ray and took his time unlocking doors and leading them to the closet-sized room containing the surveillance system. Ray scooted in first, followed by Wong, Catriona and Gray. Mr. Reiss squeezed into the chair. When he did start the replay, Gray was surprised at the high-quality footage. Most small operations didn't invest in expensive equipment. Mr. Reiss explained that he'd been a target of ATM skimmers, and he'd had no choice but to upgrade.

Last Saturday had been a busy day at the bank. The camera angle was such that the restaurant was visible from the drive-through window back to the meat smoker area. Catriona leaned forward, her body tense, as the footage changed from day to night.

"You can see my car," Ray said, pointing to the screen. "I left around nine."

They watched him walk to his Volkswagen, parked beside the vans, and leave the lot.

"There," Wong said. "Two men."

The pair—one topping the other by at least six inches—approached from the neighborhood and quickly jimmied the doors. Once inside the van, the taller man hot-wired it. The whole process took less than five minutes.

"Will you replay it?" Catriona looked over at Gray. "I think the skinny guy who held Bianca at gunpoint today is the sidekick."

They watched it again, and this time, something struck a chord. "I agree. What's more, the driver looks familiar. Mr. Reiss, would you play it again?"

He happily obliged, and Gray had him pause it so he could take a picture with his phone. Sliding out of the closet, he called the current man in charge of Winthrop security.

John answered on the third ring. "Hey, boss." He halted. "I mean, well, I guess you're not the boss anymore. I heard you'd been canned and—"

"It's okay, John. A lot has happened this week. Listen, do you know what happened to Xavier Jones?"

Catriona appeared at his elbow, her brows drawn together in question.

"Jones? He was supposed to have gone to California. Said he had a woman there."

"No one's seen or heard from him?"

"We weren't on the best of terms. I'll ask the guys, though."

"I'm going to text you an image, and I want you to tell me if you think it's him."

"You got it, boss." Another stagnant pause. "Sorry."

Gray didn't have time to ponder his professional future. He ended the call and texted John the image.

"What is it?" The furrow between her brows had grown more pronounced.

"Xavier Jones. I hired him eight months ago. He had an attitude, but he came with glowing references. More importantly, he'd been recommended by Winthrop's closest associate." If he'd refused to take him on, said associate would've been offended, and Gray would've gotten an earful from Winthrop. It was the way of top-tier society. He didn't have to like it, but he'd had to play by their rules.

"You think Xavier is the driver?"

"If it isn't him, it's his doppelgänger."

"Is he still on Wayne's payroll?"

"I fired him four months in. Not because of his lackluster performance. He was skilled, savvy and ruthless when he needed to be. But he had a problem—he disliked Winthrop. He resented his status and wealth, which he deemed excessive. If he'd kept his opinions to himself, I would've overlooked it. Unfortunately, Xavier wouldn't shut his mouth, and his constant criticisms began to affect morale."

"Did Wayne support your decision?"

"He wasn't happy about it, but he agreed it was necessary. He said he would smooth things over with his associate."

"And Xavier? How did he take being terminated?"

Gray grimaced. It had been an ugly scene that had almost turned violent. "Xavier was escorted off the premises."

"Sounds like someone with an ax to grind."

"All the while he was venting against Winthrop and rallying for the lower classes, I got the sense he was jealous."

"As in, he wouldn't mind trading places. We need to get this footage to Pike. She has the resources to run him down."

The incoming text from John confirmed Gray's suspicions. He agreed the man in the footage closely resembled Xavier.

"Would he be the type to take orders from Axel?" Catriona said.

"If he's involved, he's running the show. He chafed at authority."

"I pray this lead pans out," she said. "I can't stop thinking about her. The way she looked at me before they took her away again…" She rubbed at the middle of her forehead. "I hate feeling helpless."

"We're not helpless." He settled his hands on her shoulders. "We have Almighty God on our side."

A sigh gusted out of her. "I needed that reminder." She moved toward him as if about to rest her head on his chest, but the men left the surveillance closet just then.

Gray ignored the pang of disappointment. He needed her comforting closeness as much as she apparently craved his. But the more they gave in, the more difficult it would be when they said goodbye.

"How did she seem?" Seated across from Cat in one of JPD's private rooms, Wayne twisted the gold cuff link around and around. "Did she say how they were treating her?"

This conversation was testing her mental resolve. Wayne had pounced the moment they arrived at the station and requested to speak to her alone. If he'd commanded or bullied, she would've refused. The disintegration of this formidable man led her to believe he actually loved his daughter. The one he'd raised, not the one he'd cast aside.

Rotating the frosty soda can between her palms, she chose her words carefully. "She remained rather calm during the ordeal. I regularly deal with victims of crimes, and I have to say I'm proud of her. She showed resilience, and that will help her get through this."

He switched wrists and clamped on to the other cuff link. "Did she have any injuries?"

"I didn't observe any."

Helplessness blanketed him. "She was almost taken when she was eleven."

Cat sank against the chair. "That's not in any of the media reports."

"We worked diligently to keep it under wraps. Trying to avoid copycats." His fingers stilled, and he dropped his hands to his lap. "The man responsible was quickly apprehended. He was obsessed with Tabitha and thought he could reach her through Bianca. After that, I enhanced both the property and personal security."

"I understand that you want to focus your anger on someone, but you should reserve blame until you speak to Bianca. You wouldn't have kept Gray around for four years, much less allowed him to maintain the senior position, if he wasn't an asset to your team."

A muscle in his jaw ticked. "I'll do as you ask, if you'll do something for me in return." He reached into his jacket and retrieved a business card. "This is a reputable company. I've already submitted my DNA sample."

Cat studied the bold-type information. Once she gave the sample, the results would be official. She'd have proof of her heritage—Winthrop or not.

"Bianca always wanted a sibling," he said, his voice gruff. "Catriona, I apologize for how I've handled things, especially that infamous television interview."

She studied his features. Her gut instinct said he was sincere. Or was that just the hope of the sad little girl she'd once been?

Gray entered the room. He hadn't hidden his reservations about her going off with Wayne. His features were closed, his eyes watchful.

"Sorry to interrupt, but Pike wanted me to pass along a message. The guy you shot, Catriona, is out of surgery. She's on her way to interview him. There's a BOLO out for Xavier."

"Nothing more?" Wayne demanded.

"Afraid not."

Catriona pushed out her chair. "I have an errand to run, if you don't mind."

"Of course." Gray held the door open.

Wayne also stood up. "Are you going to the testing office?"

"As a matter of fact, I am."

"As my daughter, you'll have access to financial means and opportunities most people can't even imagine. I can provide you a lifestyle beyond compare."

"Do you think that's what I dreamed about? Money and prestige?"

His cheeks flushed, and there was a glimmer of shame in his eyes. "I can't undo the past, Catriona. I can only do what you'll allow me to, going forward."

Confusion, hurt and anger jangled up inside.

"Let's not put the cart before the horse. Right now, this is all merely speculation."

"I'm confident you're my daughter."

"Days ago, you were confident I wasn't."

Cat left before he could offer another apology. Gray's hand came to rest on her lower back and remained there until they reached the Chevelle.

"You okay?"

"Not really."

He hugged her, a quick, reassuring squeeze. Her heart lodged in her throat, and she blinked away gathering tears.

Lord, thank You for Gray. He's been the rock and support I didn't know I needed. Help me to let him go when it's time.

She asked him to drive, and Gray took her straight to the testing office and, at her request, stayed with her through the explanations and sample gathering. As they were leaving, he received a text. "It's Pike."

"Wounded guy is talking?" she asked hopefully.

"Not to law enforcement. He's asking for a lawyer. There's been a sighting of Xavier. Pike will head to the location and interview witnesses."

"I want to be there."

His mouth tipped up in a slow grin. "There's no law against taking the scenic route."

They headed toward the inland farming community of Richlands. A gas station owner had called in the tip about Xavier. Leaving the center of town behind, they drove between flat green fields.

Gray lifted a finger from the wheel. "There it is." The weathered building was located at a crossroads. A shiny new dollar store had been built across the way, and Hawk's Mechanic Shop sprawled out in the dusty lot next to that.

"I don't see Pike yet."

"Won't hurt for us to go inside and look around. Maybe see how talkative the owner is."

"I like the way you think," she said.

Like the outer facade, the interior had seen better days. A cheery welcome came from behind the massive cash register, where a woman with a cloud of silver hair sat perched on a stool.

Gray strode to the drink case while Cat pretended interest in the candy aisle. She chose a package of chewing gum and returned to the counter.

"Is that all for you?"

Cat chose a newspaper from the pile. "Have you read today's edition?"

"Front to back," she said.

"Any new information on that abduction case? I've been following the coverage on television."

The woman perked up. "They ain't doing anything except rehashing the case." She bent over the register. "Tomorrow, you'll read about this very gas station. The front page, no less."

Cat feigned surprise. "Is that so?"

"Yes, ma'am. They're looking for someone, and he just happened to come in here last night."

Her stomach dropped. "Last night?"

"I wasn't here, of course. My helper, Denise, saw him. We got to talking when I came in this morning, and she swears he was in here buying doughnuts and cigarettes."

"Huh."

The doorbell jangled, and Pike sauntered in.

She told them to wait outside while she did the official questioning. When she finally emerged, she had nothing of importance to relay. "I'm going to visit those businesses across the street and see if anyone there has useful information. You should return to Shane's. I'll let you know if I learn anything."

Disappointed, Cat got into the car and blinked back the moisture pressing against her lids. They reached the central area in Richlands, marked with chain grocery stores, popular fast-food joints and mom-and-pop shops. Gray slowed for a red light, and she scanned the strip mall boasting a nail salon, car insurance and thrift store.

"I saw something," she said, bracing her hand on the dash.

Gray stomped the brakes and whipped into the parking lot, earning an angry honk from another driver.

"I spotted a white van parked out back."

The lot was riddled with stray gravel and churned-up asphalt. Gray pulled the car close to the building and killed the engine. They exited and walked slowly to the building's corner. Pressed up against the bricks, she peeked around and surveyed the area. Mountains of discarded furniture, toys and clothes flanked either side of the rear entrance. "I can't see anyone."

A side street dissected the strip mall lot and a sprawling neighborhood.

Gray inclined his head toward the van, its front end angled toward them.

"Cover me while I get a better view."

Cat nodded and readied her weapon. He hurried past a double set of dumpsters, not faltering when a cat darted out and trotted to him. Just when he left her sight, the thrift store doors banged open and two men strolled into the lot.

Xavier.

TWENTY-FOUR

Adrenaline roared through her. Finally, here was a solid link to Bianca.

Gray reappeared and gave her a thumbs-up. Had he not heard the men?

She signaled for him to stop.

Xavier must've glimpsed him through the van's windshield. He whipped out his gun and began firing. Glass shattered. Gray didn't return fire. Why?

The man with Xavier wasn't a man after all. He was a teenager. From his expression, a scared-for-his-life teenager.

"Get down," Cat yelled, exposing her position. If the boy didn't move, she couldn't take a single shot and neither could Gray.

A bullet zinged in her direction, catching the bricks near her face. The explosion of hard material stung her cheek and neck.

Xavier darted between the dumpsters and van. Gray shifted around the hood, waiting for a clear shot. Cat sprinted across the pavement and landed in a crouch beside him.

"You're bleeding," he grunted, sparing her a concerned glance.

"A mere scratch."

Xavier made a break for the neighborhood entrance. They gave chase and were almost hit by a passing car as they crossed the street. Dogs locked behind wooden fences began to howl and bark. The risk of danger to any homeowners who happened to be outside ramped up. The memory of Sarah, the little girl who'd gotten injured at the park, cemented her resolve. They had to take this guy down before he hurt another innocent person.

Their prey wove between the older ranch-style homes, and they trailed behind, pounding down driveways and dodging garbage cans. When they encountered a group of kids playing on a backyard swing set, Cat yelled at them to go inside.

"We have to split up," she called out. "Cut him off."

Gray nodded reluctantly and pointed out his planned path. She would go straight while he ran around the side of the house, crossed through the yards and cut Xavier off.

Cat ran between two homes and had nearly cleared them when a snarling German shepherd bounded from behind a camper and blocked her way.

"Not now." She stopped short and, keeping her gaze on the dog, attempted to edge around him.

A scuffling step behind her was the only warning before a gun grip slammed into her head, right above her ear. Dazed and in pain, she stumbled. A fist followed the gun, punching with full force and catching her cheek. She fell to her knees in the grass and fought the urge to empty her stomach.

The dog's growls turned into a whimper, and he fled.

She still had her gun. Cat made to turn and aim, but Xavier's hand closed over her throat and squeezed. She clawed at his fingers. Wouldn't budge. He ripped the gun from her hand and leered at her. His vengeful eyes and cruel smile turned her blood to ice.

"We meet at last. I'm eager to get to know Michaelson's kitty-cat better." Hauling her up, he jammed his gun into her side and ordered her to walk.

Every step jarred her aching head. Where was Gray? "There's no way out of here, Xavier."

"There's always a way."

He marched her to the cul-de-sac's last house. He popped the trunk of an old Chevy the owners hadn't bothered to lock and ordered her inside.

"No."

"Do you want to make things harder for little sister?"

Cat tried to think of a plan, but her thoughts were muddled by the screaming pain.

Xavier lunged for her and seized a fistful of her hair, forcing her head back. She gasped as he brought his lips to her ear.

"I've ordered my men to keep their hands off Bianca. You go along peacefully, and I'll make sure that doesn't change."

She couldn't suppress a shiver. Going with Xavier would reunite her with Bianca. She could shield her. Keep her safe. And maybe, just maybe, help her escape.

Gray reached the cul-de-sac in time to see Xavier slam the trunk closed and jump behind the wheel. Denial threatened to immobilize him. Catriona was inside that trunk. He didn't know if she was injured. Conscious or unconscious. Had she gone willingly in a bid to help her sister?

The engine sputtered to life. He would've reached them if Xavier hadn't made a wild arc through the connecting yards and left via the neighbor's driveway.

Holstering his weapon, he called Pike. She promised to set local units in pursuit. They would rendezvous at the thrift shop. Gray ran the whole route back to the shop and was stopped by an officer already on the scene. After flashing his ID and having his story confirmed by the teenage boy, he was free to go.

"Michaelson!" Pike leaned outside her window. "We'll search together."

She didn't give him a choice. Could he blame her? Catriona would be safe right now if he'd insisted on returning to the house in Jacksonville.

When he'd buckled in and relayed the events of the last fifteen minutes, he braced for a tongue-lashing. Instead, she said, "Sergeant Baker's a fighter. You don't have to worry about her."

His lips clamped together and his fingers dug into his thighs. Catriona was now at the mercy of Xavier and his crew.

Pike sped along the road Xavier had taken. She was in near-constant communication with JPD and the Richlands police. Gray was glad he wasn't expected to speak. He wasn't sure he was capable.

He kept his eyes peeled for a sign of the maroon car. *Please, God, I can't lose her.*

Something the guy on the radio was saying broke through his tormented thoughts. He looked over at Pike, whose expression was tighter and angrier than usual.

"What?"

She held up a hand to silence him. Finally, the conversation ended. "They found the getaway car."

"And?"

"Abandoned. Xavier knew we were looking for him, so he ditched that ride and found another."

Gray's chest hurt. From the beginning, these thugs had had the upper hand. The authorities didn't know how many they were dealing with or where they were hiding the women. They were at a disadvantage, and Xavier had all the power.

Cat's body craved relief from the constant jarring and jerking. The ride seemed interminable, and she found herself both dreading and wishing for its end. What awaited her? How many associates did Xavier have and how would they treat her? She'd proved difficult to capture, and she'd personally fought with Axel and Milton. While Bianca was a young woman of means, Cat was a trained marine. That had to affect their attitude toward her.

Bianca was the bright light in this darkness.

God, please give me the strength to help her. Protect us both. Gray is probably blaming himself right now, and he needs to know this isn't his fault.

A tear squeezed past her tightly closed eyelids. All the reasons they couldn't be together seemed silly now that she wasn't sure she'd ever see him again.

No more. No more meekly accepting what life throws at you. It's time to fight for what you want, Cat. Fighting for survival was instinctual. Fighting for honor, family and love required another kind of courage.

The brakes were struck hard, and Cat slapped against the spare tire. The trunk lid popped open, and she was temporarily blinded by the late-evening sunshine. Rough hands dragged her out, and she stumbled in the dirt. There was nothing but dirt for miles. Sparse tree cover. In front of her was what looked to be an abandoned elementary school, the type from decades past that was no more than two brick rectangles welded together.

"Welcome." Xavier marched her toward a faded blue door in the building scarred with graffiti and shattered windows.

Axel emerged. His slow, triumphant grin and the way he rubbed his hands together in anticipation raised the hair on her neck.

"We've been expecting you," he said.

Cat said nothing. She had to funnel her concentration on the surroundings and possible exit routes. He took possession of her and skimmed his knuckles down her face. "You're looking the worse for wear, Sergeant."

She gritted her teeth to keep from spitting in his face. *Don't rile these snakes without just cause. Don't strike until you're reasonably sure of success.*

"Not in the mood to talk, huh? Funny, your little sister doesn't shut up."

Axel propelled her into the building. The air was dank. Grime coated the lockers and tiles. Dead beetles lay haphazardly among the dust. Classrooms in varying states of disrepair occupied both sides of the corridor. Most of the doors were missing.

A stranger stood guard outside a room at the far end. The rough character sported both a shoulder and belt holster, fitted with handguns.

"About time," he drawled, fishing out a key and unlocking the door. "Princess number one has been whining about a headache for the past hour."

"What's wrong with Bianca?" Cat asked, alarmed. "What did you do?"

Axel's fingers dug into her flesh. "We've been the perfect hosts. See for yourself." He shoved her into the squat, windowless room and slammed the door.

A single light bulb swayed from the ceiling.

"Catriona?"

Bianca sprang to her feet and threw her arms around Cat's neck. Sobs racked her frail frame. "I didn't think I'd see you again." Pulling back, she wiped her face with her sleeves.

"Are you hurt? The guard said you had a headache."

"That was a ruse to get out of this box for a few minutes. After a while, the walls start to close in and—" She cocked her head to one side. "How did they manage to capture you?"

"We had a run-in with Xavier. Bianca, how many are we dealing with?"

She grimaced. "I don't know exactly. Besides

Xavier and Axel, I've only seen the guard outside and Francis."

"Is Francis the thin one who held the gun on you?"

"Yes."

"What about Milton? Have you seen him? We call him Shaggy Hair."

Bianca's dry, cracked lips trembled. "I overheard Axel and the guard talking. They killed someone named Vera, and when he tried to get revenge, they killed him, too."

Cat couldn't say she was surprised. "I have a plan to get us out."

Instead of the enthusiastic response Cat had anticipated, Bianca backed up a step and shoved her lank hair out of her eyes. "There's no way out. We have to wait for my father to meet the ransom demands. Don't worry. He'll pay for both of us."

"There's a good chance Wayne is also my father. We've submitted DNA samples and should get the results in a few days."

Bianca hugged her again. "I've always wanted a sister," she said, fresh tears on her cheeks. "What about you? Does this news make you as happy as it makes me?"

Cat smiled. "Yes, it makes me very happy."

Her return smile was tremulous. "I guess we should get comfortable. Not easy to do on this concrete floor. They ignored my requests for a pillow and blanket."

"I have an idea," Cat said. "You pretend to be ill. I'll call for help, and when the guard comes in, I jump him and take his gun. Then we shoot our way out."

Her brow creased. "I don't know."

Cat cupped her upper arms. "I'll be frank. Hostage exchanges don't always go according to plan. Even if Wayne agrees to pay, there's no guarantee Xavier will hold up his end of the deal."

Blinking rapidly, she pressed her lips together.

"Gray and the authorities will do everything they can to find us, but it's not easy. Some of these guys are former military, and they've covered their tracks well."

"I—I don't think I can."

"You don't have to do anything except stay close to me."

When she didn't answer, Cat said, "Are you a believer, Bianca?"

"Are you asking if I believe in God?"

"Have you put your faith in Christ Jesus? Accepted His sacrifice on the cross for your sins?"

"I have," she said shyly. "My boyfriend, Lane, started attending a Christian student organization on campus last year, and he invited me to go. I've been studying my Bible. We'd planned to visit churches in our area, but then I decided to come and meet you."

"I'm glad you did." If she hadn't, Cat wouldn't have known she had a family and she wouldn't have met Gray. The thought sent a shaft of grief through her. "God is with us, Bianca. He knows what we need, when we need it. Remember that."

"He will never leave us, nor forsake us," Bianca said. "I've memorized some Scripture."

Cat gave her arms a light squeeze, then lowered her hands. "When the guard comes in, hunker over and make pitiful moaning sounds to draw him in. Once I go on the offense, stay as far away from the door as possible, okay?"

"Okay."

"Ready?"

"Yes." She shook her head from side to side. "No. Shouldn't we wait?"

"My guess is that Xavier and Axel are busy patting themselves on the back and planning their ransom call. This is the best time, trust me."

She lifted her chin. "I trust you."

Scooting to the far corner, Bianca bent over and moaned. Cat sent up a quick prayer. She wasn't in top fighting form, not after Xavier's severe treatment. At least by acting now, they had the element of surprise on their side.

Positioning herself behind where the door would swing open, she pounded on the metal. "Help! My sister's sick!" She kept pounding until she heard the knob rattle.

The goon appeared, but he stayed just inside the opening. "You're giving me a headache," he growled. "I'm not in this to play nursemaid to spoiled princesses."

"There's something wrong with her," Cat said, pointing.

Bianca moaned again and gripped her middle more tightly.

"I'm not cleaning up vomit," he warned. "Outside. Now."

Bianca staggered forward, put her hand on the wall and moaned again. When he still didn't advance, she went into a pretend fall. His instinctual reaction had him reaching for her, bringing him close enough for Cat to strike.

She landed a kick in his side that knocked him into the far wall. He recovered quickly and, growling with fury, came at her like an irate bull. She leaped out of the way. He caught her ankle, and she tripped. Before she quite knew what happened, he had her pinned on her stomach, her arms twisted painfully behind her.

"You're gonna regret that." His breath was hot and foul in her ear.

When he'd secured her wrists with zip ties, he grabbed Bianca. "Let's go, princess."

"No." Her defiance was little more than a whimper. "Please."

Cat struggled to sit up. "Take me," she demanded. "It was my idea."

He didn't listen. Snagging the chain that controlled the light, he plunged the room into darkness. The door slammed, and all she could hear were her own uneven breaths.

TWENTY-FIVE

"Ten million. That's the price tag." Gray walked a circuitous, winding path through Shane's living room.

On the other end of the call, Ryan whistled. "Winthrop will cough it up, though."

Hearing the unspoken question in his brother's voice, he said, "He's willing to pay."

Would that still have been the case if those DNA results hadn't been leaked? Or if Catriona had turned out to be another man's child?

"When's the drop?"

"Tomorrow night. 2200 hours." He clenched his fist. "I have no idea where it's taking place. Pike's determined to keep me and Winthrop out of the loop this time." If he'd been in her shoes, he would've done the same thing. The hours stretched endlessly before him. Every time his mind strayed to Catriona and Bianca and their captors, he slammed a mental gate shut. He'd seriously lose it if he followed through with that line of thinking.

"Want me to drive to Jacksonville?" Ryan quietly asked.

His brother had been subdued during this long, exhausting conversation. Gray wanted to say yes. If the drop didn't go as planned, if the women weren't rescued—

"I appreciate the offer, brother. Stay put for now."

They spoke for a few more minutes before Gray ended the call. Three hours since Cat's abduction. It felt like he'd aged one hundred years.

This place belonged to a stranger, but it was filled with memories of her. Lounging on the couch with a magazine. Scrubbing the kitchen sink until it shone. Laughing at something his brother had said, that rare sparkle in her eye and her smile unrestrained.

He sank onto the couch and buried his face in his hands. The cell's ring startled him.

"Detective, did you find something?"

"A duffel bag in the barbecue van," Pike replied. "It has motocross gear in it. Does that mean anything to you?"

He racked his brain for a connection. "No, nothing."

"I spoke with Ray, and he claims it's not his."

Pike promised to keep him updated. He sat there in the too-quiet house, going over the case from start to finish. Then he zeroed in on something Bianca had said in the car. She'd heard revving sounds. Revving, as in dirt bikes?

He did a quick internet search for area motocross tracks and off-road trails. There was only one in the greater Jacksonville area, and it was located in the south, toward Wilmington. Xavier would need somewhere isolated to hold the women. A personally owned track not open to the general public would be a better fit. He'd been spotted in the Richlands area. Another search yielded a single motocross shop in a small community between Richlands and the interstate. He tried to reach someone, then realized the shop was closed for the night.

Locating the social media page, he sent a quick message to the owner, pretending to be a motocross enthusiast interested in a challenging, off-the-books course.

A half hour crawled past. Then another. The moment his phone alerted him to the response, he opened the message with trembling fingers. There was only one track like the one he was looking for, the man had replied. He gave Gray the address but advised him that the track owner was out of town.

Out of town? Perfect for Xavier and his crew. Grabbing his keys, he texted Pike the address.

He reached the location in just under twenty minutes, somehow managing to avoid a speeding ticket. It was nearing midnight, so traffic was light. Thick stands of pines lined the road. He wedged the car between them and, gun in hand, hiked along the meandering dirt trail that substituted for a driveway. The property appeared to be deserted. No structures broke up the acres of grass and pines. Using a flashlight, he followed the path as it curved around another patch of trees. In the distance, atop a slight swell of land, sat a snakelike building with broken-out windows for teeth, yellow squares of light forming a strange pattern. The truck that had bombarded them in the city was parked outside.

Gray hit the flashlight's off button and used a nearby tree for support. He'd found them. He stood there for a full minute, debating whether or not to wait for authorities. The decision was taken out of his hands when he heard a bloodchilling scream.

Sticking to the shadows until he came even with the building, he darted across the clearing and crept past the first darkened classroom. Yet another scream pierced the night, and it was coming from the next room over.

Edging to the nearest window, he peeked through the filmy glass. Xavier held a gun to Bianca's head and commanded her to scream again. When the earsplitting sound died off, he chuckled and spoke to someone Gray couldn't see.

"That should get under the marine's skin."

His frantic pulse slowed somewhat. They were playing mind games with Catriona.

Bianca looked much as she had at the fairgrounds. Disheveled and dirty, but uninjured. Arms hugging her middle, she trained her gaze on the floor. The men left her. Gray tapped on the glass. She flinched. He tapped again and, when she'd inched to the window, slowly revealed his presence, his finger pressed to his lips.

Her eyes went wide, and her face contorted with relief.

"Can you crank one of these panels open?" He spoke only loud enough for her to hear him.

Darting glances at the door, she walked along the wall and tried the old-fashioned rotating cranks. Gnawing on her lip, she shook her head.

He scanned the panes until he found one with a crack. "Take off that jacket, wrap your hand in it and bust out the glass."

The dirt would mute the sound, and he could reach in and get the rusted cranks to work. Bianca reluctantly removed the jacket and, creating a wrap around her hand, gingerly tapped the glass.

Gray gritted his teeth. "Again," he urged. "Harder."

Five attempts later, the glass gave way. Reaching in, Gray closed his fingers around the crank and applied all of his might to jar it. The window panel creaked as it slowly opened. Bianca bounced on her tiptoes.

As soon as it was wide enough, she vaulted through. Gray almost didn't catch her in time.

"Listen, B. Take my phone to those trees over there and call the police. Tell them where you're hiding. Where are they holding Catriona?"

"I'm not leaving either of you."

"You wouldn't be leaving. You'd be nearby." And out of the way.

Her eyes flashed. "I've got to be brave, like my sister."

"B—"

The doorknob rattled. Gray seized her hand, and they broke into a run.

Cat was deep in prayer when the door burst open, and Xavier grabbed her.

"Where's Bianca?"

Not bothering to give her an answer, he propelled her along the long corridor and into the central cafeteria area, which wasn't much larger than her rental cottage. Her ears detected the faint whir of sirens. Had the police located their hideout at long last?

Axel emerged from the kitchen, and Xavier waved his weapon to the double doors that emptied into the next building.

"Check it out."

Cat twisted her wrists, testing the zip ties. They weren't budging.

A gun report blasted through the other building, and Xavier tried and failed to reach his cohort by phone.

"The police are coming," she said. "You should leave us. You—"

"You're not in charge, Sergeant," he growled. Sweat beaded on his forehead. His leg bobbed.

If only her hands weren't bound, she could use his distraction to her advantage.

There was a ping on a window to their right, and he pivoted and took a shot. Glass rained on the cement tiles. Cat flinched and would've hit the ground, but he prevented her.

"Move."

Hustling her to the same doors that Axel had disappeared through, he shoved her in first. "Axel?"

There was no answer from the bald man. No sight of him, either. Xavier was rigid with tension. Pivoting back, they retraced their steps and went outside, where his truck was parked. Light spilling from the cafeteria and other rooms illuminated the immediate area around the building.

The truck engine roared, and the headlights temporarily blinded them. A form entered the cone of light, and Cat gasped.

Gray leveled his weapon at Xavier. "Let her

go. Axel and his buddy are down for the count, and there's no one else to hide behind."

There was a third man, the one who'd guarded Bianca. Before she could warn Gray, Xavier spoke.

"Michaelson. Still playing the white-knight routine, I see." He dug the gun barrel into Cat's temple, and she winced. "You're sure you don't want to join forces? We could split the ransom money fifty-fifty. Live a life of leisure south of the border."

"Not interested."

"Worth a try." Xavier shrugged. "Tell Bianca to get out of my truck."

Out of the shadows, the guard slammed into Gray. He collided with the truck, regrouped and engaged in hand-to-hand combat.

Xavier began to drag Cat away. The engine revved, and the truck lurched forward. They leaped closer to the building, but Bianca didn't let up on the gas. Cat hurled her body into Xavier. He tripped and hit the ground, pulling her down with him, using her as a shield.

The massive grille bore down on them, the thick, oversize tires ready to crush them into the dirt. Cat screamed Bianca's name. Gray's voice penetrated the deafening rumble. Just as the chrome was close enough for Cat to see her reflection, the truck stopped.

Gray reached into the space, pulled Cat to

safety and leveled his weapon at Xavier. The sirens were almost deafening now.

"You're done, Xavier," Gray shouted. "Toss your weapon, or I'll have Bianca flatten you."

Hatred gleaming in his eyes, Xavier did as Gray instructed and remained on the ground. Patrol cars surrounded the school, and the SWAT tank truck released a tide of geared-for-battle members.

The moment Xavier was no longer a threat and Cat's ties were cut, she threw her arms around Gray. He hugged her close and buried his face in her hair. Relief and joy built to a crescendo, until she almost couldn't contain it. Seconds later, another set of arms circled them both, and they lifted their heads to see Bianca grinning at them. Tears shone on her face.

"You were very brave," Cat told her.

"I learned by example."

Pike intruded upon their happy reunion with rapid-fire questions and a scolding for Gray. He was supposed to have waited for her.

"Well, it ended well enough," Pike said. "You're headed back to Chicago?"

He shot Cat a sideways glance. "That's the plan."

Cat stewed over his answer while the paramedics examined her. The person she once was would've accepted his decision without a word of complaint. She would've said goodbye, even though his absence would ruin her. Not this time.

Once the perps were secured and whisked to either the hospital or JPD, Wayne was given access to the property. His reaction to seeing Bianca almost convinced Cat that he possessed a heart.

Gray walked away from the ambulance and slid his hand into hers. Tugging her away from the activity, he led her to the outer reaches of light.

"I don't want you to go," she blurted, almost dizzy from fear of rejection. "I know you have a life in Chicago, but I'm asking you to consider a change."

His eyes lightened, and his smile warmed her to her toes. "What are you trying to say, Catriona? You like me?"

Emotion lodged in her throat. "More than like."

His palm cupped her cheek. "You admire me?"

"More."

Gripping his shoulder, she leaned in and touched her lips to his. He sucked in a quick breath, then welcomed her closer. When she broke away, he wasn't as calm and collected as he'd been before. Good.

"I love you, Gray." The words whooshed out of her. "I've never said that to anyone in my life."

His arms circled her. "I'm a fortunate man," he said quietly, somberly. "I won't ever forget that your trust and your love are priceless gifts. I love you, Catriona Baker, and I will follow you wherever the Marines send you."

EPILOGUE

Six months later

"May I have this dance?"

Cat glanced at her friend Olivia. "What do you think? Should I accept?"

Chuckling, Olivia rested her hand atop her rounded belly. "It is tradition for the bride and groom to dance on their wedding day. No one else will until you've had your whirl around the floor."

Brady slid his arm around his heavily pregnant wife. "I'm hoping for a dance of my own," he quipped.

"At this point, it's going to be more of a sway-in-one-place deal."

Brady kissed her cheek. "As long as you're in my arms, I'm happy."

Gray, sleek and sophisticated in his black tuxedo, held out his hand. "Well?"

Looking around, she could see the guests watching and waiting. Gray's parents and twin brothers looked on with happy smiles. Her friend Stacie had taken leave in order to be here.

Cat swallowed her nerves and placed her hand in his. "Let's hope those lessons paid off."

"Follow my lead," he whispered, pulling her into his sheltering embrace and leading her in the steps they'd practiced.

Cat locked her gaze on her husband's face. *Husband.* The word threatened to choke her up.

His fingers flexed on her waist. "There's a set of exit doors on our right. I'll whirl you right out onto the patio if that's what you want."

"I love you."

The concern in his eyes morphed into that warm beacon, that lighthouse-on-the-shore that called her home. He'd fallen in love with her during her lowest of lows, which meant he wasn't going to ditch her at the first sign of trouble. He was in this for the long haul.

"I want to be right here, in your arms, always," she murmured, stroking his cheek.

Gray held her even tighter and finished out the dance without another word. She knew what he was thinking. He was counting the minutes until they departed the airport for their honeymoon. Fourteen days of Hawaiian sun, sand and blissful privacy.

Over his shoulder, she wagged her fingers at Audrey and Julian. The surgical nurse and Force Recon instructor often joined her, Gray, Olivia and Brady for board game and pizza nights. Last week, they'd announced they were finally expecting after more than a year of trying. Audrey was practically glowing, and Julian was already in full-on protection mode.

"Cade and Tori sent a gift and their regrets. They can't get away until summer." The couple, whom she'd met during their visits with Olivia and Brady, were stationed at Camp Pendleton.

"Maybe Cade will be reassigned to the East Coast soon."

"By then, we could be elsewhere," she reminded him.

His smile made her knees go weak. "As long as I'm with you, I'll be happy."

The music slowed, and as other couples joined them on the dance floor, she rested her head on his shoulder. Gratitude prevented her from speaking. Gray had spent the last months building his own security firm, hiring men and women to work in the Jacksonville and Wilmington areas. In the event Cat received orders to relocate, he could operate the firm remotely and recruit employees in their new city.

"Ready for some fresh air?" he whispered.

"Are you trying to get me alone, Mr. Michaelson?"

"Yes."

Laughing, she took his hand. As they reached

the buffet table, Staff Sergeant Taube blocked their way.

"I'm sorry to intrude, but I've had news on your case."

Gray's hold on her hand tightened, and Cat's stomach did a somersault. Shortly after Xavier and his crew had been taken into custody, she'd initiated the investigation proceedings into the Okinawa incident. Taube had been her initial go-to, and he'd proved invaluable in making sure the case traveled up the chain of command.

"If it's bad news, it can wait until after our honeymoon."

Taube shook his head. "During the course of the investigation, one of Craft's cohorts started spilling secrets and names. Lots of names. You'll see this in the news in the coming days."

"Did Craft admit his guilt?"

"He's still in denial mode, but his quarters are being raided as we speak. They'll find the evidence you need to clear your name."

Overcome, Cat hugged him.

He patted her shoulder. "Um, you're welcome?"

Blushing, she released him. "Thank you, sir."

Gray shook his hand. "We can never repay you."

"This is all due to Sergeant Baker's commitment to truth and her outstanding courage." Taking a cup of punch from the nearby table, he inclined his head. "I'm honored to serve with you, Baker."

Cat sent up a prayer of thanksgiving. Her reputation would finally be restored, the blot on her name wiped out.

"You'll have to get used to calling her Sergeant Michaelson from now on," Gray reminded him.

Bianca chose that moment to introduce herself to Taube. Even though she'd moved to Jacksonville a month after her abductors' arrests, she hadn't lost her fascination for the marines. She and Lane had decided against trying to make a go of a long-distance relationship.

When Taube had escaped to his table, Bianca shrugged and grinned. "What? He's not only good-looking, he's a nice guy. You can't tell me he's too old for me, either."

Gray rolled his eyes, and Cat laughed. "She's right, you know."

"You should be concentrating on your course work," he said.

"Great. He's switched from imperious bodyguard to bossy brother-in-law." Leaning in, she bussed his cheek. "I still love you, though."

Cat relished the teasing affection between the two most important people in her life. Bianca had refused to return to Chicago after her ordeal. She had enrolled in general courses at the local community college and volunteered at the animal shelter. Since moving into an apartment with Bianca, Cat had gotten a crash course in sisterhood. While they'd had wildly different upbringings, their personalities meshed well. The biggest hurdle was getting Bianca to remember that, unlike at the Chicago mansion, there were no maids to clean the dishes or wash the towels.

Gray had rented a house a mile away, and they'd spent most of their free time together. Many days, Bianca had joined them.

"Our father wants to speak to you," Bianca said, her expression turning solemn. "He's waiting outside."

Gray accompanied her as far as the door. Cat walked into the unseasonably warm late-February day. Wayne waited with a small package in his hands. He'd attended the ceremony at her request but had remained on the periphery. She wasn't ready for him to play a significant role in her life.

He smiled and offered her the gift. As she pulled away the paper, her breath caught in her throat. It was a framed photograph of a smiling, obviously pregnant Tabitha.

"She was expecting me?"

"It's the only photograph I took of her during that time." There was both sorrow and regret in his voice. "I can't give you back those years, Catriona. I can't ask Tabitha's forgiveness, but I wanted to tell you face-to-face that I'm sorry for what I did."

Cat lifted her gaze and saw proof of his sincerity. In the beginning, he'd tried to win her over with lavish gifts and offers to buy her a house, a car or a vacation. When she'd refused, he'd left her alone for the most part. Occasionally, he'd sent old photographs of her mother or personal items…jewelry, trinkets, signed albums. When it had come time to plan her wedding, she'd known she wanted him there.

"I've been searching the Scriptures lately for verses about forgiveness," she told him. "God brought Gray and Bianca into my life for a specific purpose. He also brought you."

His lips parted, and hope flared in his eyes.

"It won't be easy for me to trust you, but I'd like for us to get to know each other better."

"I'd like nothing better."

Gray emerged from the building, and Wayne excused himself.

"What did he want?"

"To give me this."

Gray examined the photo and slid his arm around her waist. "She would've loved you as much as I do."

She leaned into his side. "Tell me again about the time she left a concert and demanded you find her the best ice cream shop in the city."

He chuckled. "Tabitha had a hankering for something with caramel and chocolate that night…"

Cat listened to him recount the now-familiar story. Gray's and Bianca's memories brought her mother to life in her mind, a gift she would treasure always.

"It's amazing, isn't it?" she asked, taking in the stars studding the night sky.

He pressed a kiss to her hair. "What's that?"

"God used a terrible situation to bring me my heart's desire. I have a husband, a sister and a father. I have a forever family."

* * * * *

If you enjoyed this story,
look for these other books by Karen Kirst:

Explosive Reunion
Intensive Care Crisis
Danger in the Deep

Dear Reader,

Thank you for spending time in my fictional world! I hope you enjoyed Cat and Gray's wild adventure. This story had quite a few twists, and it was a challenge to keep them all straight in my head. I'm sad to say goodbye to this military miniseries. It was fun to revisit Camp Lejeune, where my husband was stationed, as well as the surrounding areas. I used to buy groceries at the New River Air Station commissary, take my kids swimming at the base pool and have picnics at the marina. Like Gray and Cat, we took advantage of the base theater. Wilmington was a wonderful place to spend time, especially the downtown district. I shopped in the multilevel shopping complex, called the Cotton Exchange, and passed lovely afternoons at the now-closed waterfront tearoom. The children's museum is also a must if you have little ones. If you get a chance to visit, I encourage you to do so.

For my next series, I'm turning my attention to the brave police officers who make up mounted patrol units. I hope you'll join me and a whole batch of new characters. If you'd like to learn more about my historical and suspense books, please visit my website at www.karenkirst.com. I'm also active on Facebook. You can email me at karenkirst@live.com.

God Bless,
Karen Kirst

Get 4 FREE REWARDS!

We'll send you 2 FREE Books plus 2 FREE Mystery Gifts.

Harlequin Heartwarming Larger-Print books will connect you to uplifting stories where the bonds of friendship, family and community unite.

FREE
Value Over
$20

YES! Please send me 2 FREE Harlequin Heartwarming Larger-Print novels and my 2 FREE mystery gifts (gifts worth about $10 retail). After receiving them, if I don't wish to receive any more books, I can return the shipping statement marked "cancel." If I don't cancel, I will receive 4 brand-new larger-print novels every month and be billed just $5.74 per book in the U.S. or $6.24 per book in Canada. That's a savings of at least 21% off the cover price. It's quite a bargain! Shipping and handling is just 50¢ per book in the U.S. and $1.25 per book in Canada.* I understand that accepting the 2 free books and gifts places me under no obligation to buy anything. I can always return a shipment and cancel at any time. The free books and gifts are mine to keep no matter what I decide.

161/361 HDN GNPZ

Name (please print)

Address   Apt. #

City   State/Province   Zip/Postal Code

Email: Please check this box ☐ if you would like to receive newsletters and promotional emails from Harlequin Enterprises ULC and its affiliates. You can unsubscribe anytime.

Mail to the **Reader Service:**
IN U.S.A.: P.O. Box 1341, Buffalo, NY 14240-8531
IN CANADA: P.O. Box 603, Fort Erie, Ontario L2A 5X3

Want to try 2 free books from another series! Call 1-800-873-8635 or visit www.ReaderService.com.

THE WESTERN HEARTS COLLECTION!

19 FREE BOOKS in all!

COWBOYS. RANCHERS. RODEO REBELS.
Here are their charming love stories in one prized Collection:
51 emotional and heart-filled romances that capture the majesty and rugged beauty of the American West!

YES! Please send me **The Western Hearts Collection** in Larger Print. This collection begins with 3 FREE books and 2 FREE gifts in the first shipment. Along with my 3 free books, I'll also get the next 4 books from The Western Hearts Collection, in LARGER PRINT, which I may either return and owe nothing, or keep for the low price of $5.45 U.S./$6.23 CDN each plus $2.99 U.S./$7.49 CDN for shipping and handling per shipment*. If I decide to continue, about once a month for 8 months I will get 6 or 7 more books but will only need to pay for 4. That means 2 or 3 books in every shipment will be FREE! If I decide to keep the entire collection, I'll have paid for only 32 books because 19 books are FREE! I understand that accepting the 3 free books and gifts places me under no obligation to buy anything. I can always return a shipment and cancel at any time. My free books and gifts are mine to keep no matter what I decide.

☐ 270 HCN 5354   ☐ 470 HCN 5354

Name (please print)

Address   Apt. #

City   State/Province   Zip/Postal Code

Mail to the **Reader Service:**
IN U.S.A.: P.O. Box 1341, Buffalo, N.Y. 14240-8531
IN CANADA: P.O. Box 603, Fort Erie, Ontario L2A 5X3